D0572478

SONGLANDS

SONGLANDS

John Feffer

Haymarket Books
Chicago, Illinois

Published in 2021 by
Haymarket Books
P.O. Box 180165
Chicago, IL 60618
773-583-7884
www.haymarketbooks.org
info@haymarketbooks.org

ISBN: 978-1-64259-464-5

Distributed to the trade in the US through Consortium Book Sales
and Distribution (www.cbsd.com) and internationally through
Ingram Publisher Services International (www.ingramcontent.com).

This book was published with the generous support of Lannan
Foundation and Wallace Action Fund.

Special discounts are available for bulk purchases by organizations
and institutions. Please call 773-583-7884 or email info@
haymarketbooks.org for more information.

Cover design by Jamie Kerry.

Printed in Canada by union labor.

Library of Congress Cataloging-in-Publication data is available.

10 9 8 7 6 5 4 3 2 1

For my teachers

Chapter 1

It happened as I was cutting my husband's ties in half.

More precisely, it happened when—the scissors midway through some very soft and very expensive black nanofabric—I was thinking, "My god, is this a cliché?" It felt so good to destroy this intimate part of my husband's wardrobe, but I needed to put down the scissors immediately if I was only going through the motions I'd seen in a movie or read about in a book. It was bad enough for clichés to creep into my writing. It was much worse to become a cliché myself.

That's when an unusual knock on the front door interrupted my tie-cutting as well as my thoughts about tie-cutting.

The interruption was unusual for two reasons. Our building has a very effective security system, and our neighbors almost never come over without messaging first. The knocks, meanwhile, were slow and precisely spaced, as if a giant, aging woodpecker had perched on the doorknob. It was an absurd image. There hadn't been woodpeckers of any size in South Brussels for years, not even in our Zone Verte.

I summoned my virtual monitor. In the screen that opened at eye level, a young woman stood at attention, her posture like that of a military officer. Her head was shaven, her skin as dark as real Flemish hot chocolate. Strange tattoos covered her neck. Her blue eyes were flecked with gold. Even in the harsh LED light of the hallway, she was very beautiful.

I tapped the intercom button. "Yes?"

"My name is Karyn. I have a message from your mother."

"I doubt it."

She pulled an envelope from a knapsack dangling in her hand and held it up to the camera. "It is a written message."

"How did you get into the building?"

"I had a conversation with the security system."

I snorted. "A conversation?"

"We came to an understanding."

Perhaps she was crazy. She claimed to talk with machines. She carried a message from a woman who was missing and presumed dead. "And how could you possibly have a message from my mother?"

"We traveled together to the Arctic."

I stiffened. "When was that?"

"Ten months ago," Karyn said.

My mother is—or, perhaps, was—a glaciologist. When I was a child, she made many trips to what she called the "frostlands." As soon as she'd moved to an intentional community in her early fifties, those research trips ended. Ten months ago, however, my mother set off on a preposterous mission to "save the world" by stimulating the regrowth of the polar ice cap using some scientific stratagem that I can't even pretend to understand. Having seen no news reports of enormous changes in the Arctic, I assumed she'd failed and said my silent goodbye to her. I'd also cried, less for my octogenarian mother perhaps than for me, for being newly orphaned.

"Where is she now?" I asked.

"She is still there."

A little flame of hope ignited inside me. "Is she. . . alive?"

Karyn began to do something quite odd. Her gaze faltered, and she looked away from the camera. Then she started to slap her palm against her forehead. "I do not know," she groaned.

"It's okay," I said quickly. "Hey, stop it!"

She ignored me and continued the strange repetitive motion. I rushed to open the door, if only to get her to stop hitting herself. Before this bald woman knocked herself out, I wanted to pry out every last detail about my mother.

Lowering her hand, Karyn paused as if to catch her breath. Now that she was only inches away from me across the threshold, I could see just how striking she was. Her skin was flawless, her eyes mesmerizing. She held out the letter. "Your mother told me to give you this, Aurora."

My gaze was drawn not to the letter but to the hand holding it, which was missing a finger. Now everything began to make sense. In the space where the pinkie would have been was a stitched flap that was almost skin. Its corrugated edge told me that Karyn was not human.

Once I'd ushered her into the living room, I could see the other signs. Her chest didn't rise and fall with her breathing. She didn't blink. All of the automatic functions that make us human are wholly absent in automatons—a lovely poetic irony that I suspect is lost on the tech crowd.

Karyn handed me the envelope and placed her knapsack on the couch. "It took me a long time to get here. I thought that one boat was going to Antwerp but it went to Archangel instead. Then there was the kidnapping in Crimea where I lost my finger. Perhaps I can tell you these stories later, if you are interested."

On the front of the envelope, an oblong of shiny aluminum, was written, "For my daughter." On the back was a scribbled addendum. "PS: Take Karyn immediately to your closest service center. Read this later! Hurry!"

"Are you . . . sick?" I asked her.

Karyn raised her hand to look at the absent finger. "It's nothing."

"My mother seemed to think you need to go to the service center right away."

"Service center?" Karyn seemed genuinely confused.

"For servicing."

"I don't understand."

"Like a doctor," I explained.

"Oh, yes, a doctor. Perhaps. For a general check-up. I've been traveling for a long time. And I'm a little tired."

I'm not the kind of person to employ an AI. I prefer to do my own housework. When my boys were babies, I resisted hiring a neuro-nanny. I'm a rather traditional sociology professor, so I suppose it goes with the territory. I read actual books. I write poetry. I have retinal implants but haven't used them in a while, and I'm not even sure they still work. My husband, an ever more fervent fan of the avant-garde the older he gets, scorns what he calls my "ludicrous Luddism" and is constantly on the lookout for the latest thing. I am, alas, increasingly *démodé*. Behind the curve. An old thing.

All of which meant that I didn't know the location of the nearest service center. I grabbed my purse and escorted Karyn out the door. "Hurry," my mother had written. It was just like her to order me around this way, even from a great distance, even possibly from beyond the grave. She was never one for ambiguity or ambivalence. To her, the world was black and white, and she knew exactly where she stood in it.

"Can you bring us to the nearest service center?" I asked my new robot acquaintance as we stepped outside into the warm October day.

"I'm having some difficulty accessing the virtual map of this city."

"What about just an old-fashioned web map?"

"Not working."

Karyn was certainly artificial, but the jury was still out on whether she possessed much in the way of intelligence.

I steered us in the direction of Tech Town, the area of South Brussels where I was confident we'd find a service center. It was a short walk through a safe neighborhood. Tech Town itself, though still in the Zone Verte, was dicier, so my plan was to choose the first respectable-looking establishment we encountered.

"Why don't you know if my mother is alive or not?" I asked Karyn.

"She was alive when I departed. I left her with all the food."

"Very generous of you." Since sarcasm is useless with AIs, I should have kept my mouth shut.

"We must respect our elders," Karyn said. "But winter was close. And she is old."

"Then why did you leave her behind?"

"She insisted."

"Why?"

"Because the work was not done. And winter was close."

"But why leave her at all?"

"She insisted. And she is old."

"What difference does her age make?" I asked, exasperated.

"We must respect our elders."

This conversation with Karyn reminded me of a *pantoum*, a poem that repeated lines from one quatrain to the next in different order. *Pantoums* can be beautiful and incantatory. This, however, was simply maddening. I longed to open the envelope and search my mother's words for answers to my questions, but I dutifully followed her orders.

The problem was Karyn. She was slowing down.

"Do you need to rest?" I asked her.

"I am fine."

"My mother said this was urgent. Can you hurry up?"

"I am walking as quickly as I can."

She wasn't. She was strolling. She didn't look sick or debilitated. She looked distracted, like a tourist taking in her new surroundings.

"Can you check your . . . settings or whatever?"

"My settings?" Karyn cocked an eyebrow.

"Look, I don't know very much about AI, so—"

"Why are you talking about artificial intelligence?"

I wondered if I'd made some kind of linguistic blunder akin to using gendered pronouns with a nonbinary person. Maybe it was no longer polite to refer to AIs as AIs.

"I just mean, can you do some kind of internal check of your functions."

"I am fine," she insisted.

When we entered Tech Town, she was barely moving forward. So I dragged her into the first service center that appeared, even though the look of the place was less than promising. It was in need of a paint job or, better yet, a tear-down. "Automat 43," read the sign above the door, though the "mat" was barely visible.

We waited a few seconds before I realized that the door did not open automatically. To enter, I had to push hard with my shoulder. At first, I suspected shoddy construction. Then I looked down and discovered a body on the floor near the entrance, lying with its legs bent back at an impossible angle. It was twitching spasmodically as if suffering from a seizure.

I helped Karyn maneuver around the defective machine to enter what looked like the innards of some old-fashioned computer, with coils of tubing on the floor, skeins of wire and cord hanging from the ceiling, and circuit boards of every shape and size stacked like shingling against the walls. Behind the counter were bins of hands and feet and various joints. None of them looked new.

We'd ended up in a chop shop, where electronics die and are reborn.

A supreme example of this commitment to recycling now stood facing us behind the counter. It was an older model AI with piebald skin and a vaguely humanoid face that only gestured in the direction of a nose. It had one white hand and one black one, and it was of indeterminate gender.

"Can I help you?" it asked in English with an American accent. It must have scanned my implants to determine my birthplace.

I looked back at the twitching body.

"Don't mind him," the AI said. "That was my assistant. He stopped working during his BIOS update. He just needs a few adjustments."

"That doesn't give me a lot of confidence in your workmanship."

"Fixing my assistant is not my number-one priority," the AI replied.

"What about sweeping him up and depositing him in the dustbin?"

"Did you come here just to insult us?"

I took a deep breath. Thanks probably to bored coders, some AIs have been programmed with what passes for a sense of humor. "Can you do a diagnostic or whatever it is you do on my . . . friend here?"

"With pleasure. Please step behind the counter." It gestured for Karyn to stand beneath what looked like a grid of ancient fluorescent lights. As soon as she was in place, the lights began to flash, and a cicada whir filled the air.

"What a strange place this is," Karyn said as she looked at the light fixture above her head.

I pulled out my mother's letter with the intention of reading it during the tests. Before I'd even extracted the single piece of paper from the envelope, however, the whir died away.

"All done," the AI said.

I stepped to the counter. "I guess that means it's good news."

"No news is good news," the AI said, bending down to place a charging panel near Karyn's shin. "And unfortunately I have news for you."

"What's the problem?"

"You had 45 seconds."

"Before?"

"Irreversible model decay."

"Meaning?"

"Loss of all memory."

"Surely we could have. . . rebooted."

"All systems were reconfigured to protect core memory."

"I don't know what you're talking about. Karyn, can you translate?"

Karyn turned her gold-flecked blue eyes lazily toward me. She again tried to hit herself on the forehead, this time in slow motion.

"Please stop doing that," I said sharply. "Can you tell me what's in that memory of yours that's so special?"

"I cannot distinguish between what is special and what is not special," she said in a drowsy tone. "Do you know what's special in your memory?"

I appealed to the AI. "Can *you* tell me?"

"If you share the password."

"Karyn?" I asked without much hope.

Karyn was busy looking at her shin.

"There might have been damage," the AI said, running a sensor over Karyn's midsection.

"Is that why she hits herself?"

"I wouldn't know. It might be H-RAM."

"Please?"

"Transfer of short-term memory to long-term storage. Similar to your hippocampus."

"When will you know for sure?"

The AI considered me with its unsettling, circular eyes. "Do we ever know anything for sure?"

"Listen, Socrates—"

It interrupted me, "We'll know more after a full recharge."

"And how long will this recharging take?"

"It's a new model," the AI said. "One hour."

"Do I need to stay here? I was in the middle of a very important job."

Karyn was patting her body. "I must have left my bag at your apartment."

"We can do a general tune-up," the AI said, filling out an order. "Finger replacement. New lenses."

"You're trying to upsell me," I said.

The AI shrugged. "Your 'friend' is missing a finger. That is a basic repair."

The body of the assistant AI, still twitching on the ground behind me, gave off several alarming squeaks.

I hesitated.

"This is a quality shop," the AI said, oblivious to the contrary evidence. "But you can always risk irreversible model decay by moving your 'friend' somewhere else."

"I need to go," Karyn said, looking around. "I need to get my bag. It is very important that I get my bag. Immediately."

"Don't worry," I told her. "I can get your bag."

"It's . . . it's . . ." Karyn blinked a few times. "It's too late. It's gone."

"Nonsense, I'll get your bag." I turned to the AI in exasperation. "Do what you have to do."

"We require payment in full up front."

Grumbling, I thrust out my wrist and heard the click of a credit withdrawal.

Karyn glanced at the supine body of the assistant as if that would be her fate as well. Her frightened look reminded me of the first time I dropped my sons at kindergarten.

"Why are you leaving me here with these . . . things?" she asked.

"It's for your own good," I said, before delivering the *pantoum*'s final line. "Winter is close, I am old, and I insist."

Karyn nodded gravely as I took my leave.

In two hours, I figured I could read my mother's letter, cut the rest of my husband's ties in half, retrieve Karyn's bag, and perhaps even squeeze in a little lunch. I hurried out of Tech Town and retraced my steps to the apartment.

But my apartment was no longer there.

Chapter 2

My apartment had been removed from the third floor of the building as cleanly as a diseased molar from a jaw.

At first, I thought I'd been tricked by the sun or a confluence of shadows. But as I approached, I saw that nothing remained of my residence and possessions except a sprinkling of glass on the sidewalk outside and the mural of a jungle scene I'd painted long ago on the wall of the children's bedroom. Even from the street the blazing eyes of the predator were still visible: *Tyger, Tyger burning bright, in the forests of the night*. . .

Our apartment had overlooked this quiet, tree-lined street. In the now exposed hallway some eight meters off the ground, a neighbor was standing as if at the back of a cave, talking to a trio of police officers. Glowing orange cones blocked off the sidewalk, so I took shelter from the sun with a scattering of onlookers under the awning of a convenience store across the street.

Even with a brick wall against my back, I felt a strange vertigo, as if I were three flights up on the edge of my now-missing apartment, reaching for something, anything, to steady myself. My children were safely at a boarding school in the Swiss Alps. My husband was away on a "business trip" to a "conference" in Barcelona. Everything else: gone. I reminded myself that my class lectures, my poems, the family videos were all backed up in the Cloud. But other things were irretrievable. For some reason, my first thought was of a nineteenth-century corkscrew from France, an odd wedding gift from a distant relative that had proven quite useful until wine became too expensive to buy. Gone, too, were my shoes, my jewelry, the black cocktail dress my mother had given me so many years ago to wear to my poetry readings.

My husband's ties, which I'd been in the middle of carefully cutting in half: atomized as well. Poof!

I giggled involuntarily.

I should have felt unmitigated horror at what had just happened to my life, yet I felt giddily liberated. If I'd been a bolder person, I would already have done the deed myself. Yet the anger I possessed was a paralyzing one that pushed and pulled, that was simultaneously centrifugal and centripetal, an anger that held me for years in a geosynchronous orbit around a thoroughly conventional life. Perhaps it had somehow manifested itself in a singular psychokinetic burst that had torched the apartment. Or maybe there'd been a gas leak in the kitchen. I couldn't imagine anything else that could have erased my apartment and yet left everything surrounding it intact.

"That was zip-zap," one of a pair of teenagers just to my left said in French. In the hot South Brussels autumn, he wore only a loincloth. His skin was tinted robin's egg blue. "Never saw anything like it. I mean, in meatspace."

"Total surgical strike," said the other, in a matching loincloth but mauve from head to toe with a spiky bird of paradise between his shoulder blades. He spoke in a loud voice, as if he hoped that other people on the sidewalk would ask him for more of his insights.

I obliged. "What was it?"

"Drone," the blue one said.

"*Drones*," the mauve one corrected him. "Total swarm."

Blue shrugged. "Probably a football club."

"Not here in Zone Verte," Mauve disagreed. "Must have been a political hit."

"What do you mean?" I asked.

Mauve shrugged as if what he'd said was self-explanatory.

"What kind of political hit?" I pressed.

"They took out a sleeper cell," Mauve responded. "I heard a cop say that."

I couldn't stop myself. "Sleeper cell? In this neighborhood? That's ridiculous!"

Blue looked at me suspiciously as he elbowed Mauve.

"That's what the cop said!" Mauve repeated. "And you said that—"

Blue corralled his friend and set off quickly, whispering, "You know her? You ever seen her before? Why can't you keep your mouth shut when. . ."

I'd been stupid myself. I interviewed people for a living, so I knew exactly how to keep informants talking. And at that moment what I needed more than anything else was information.

Of course, I knew the basics. Both Flanders and Wallonia were popular haunts for Sleepers, the underground followers of a virtual caliphate. They set off bombs. They divided into smaller factions and fought one another. In the Wild West of South Brussels' Zone Rouge, they squared off against the ultranationalist paramilitary forces known as the White Tigers. It was the same story throughout Europe and increasingly around the world: fanatical adherents of a religious ideology versus fanatical adherents of a political ideology. This is what happened when, as Yeats famously put it in "The Second Coming," the "centre cannot hold." A blood-rimmed tide had indeed submerged the planet.

There was no reason, however, for either religious or political fanatics to have ordered a hit on me or my family. I'm an obscure academic and an even more obscure poet. As for my husband, the only person who would order a hit on him would be me because of his trips to nonexistent conferences to "give papers" with "colleagues in the field." I knew exactly what he was giving (and getting from) colleagues in the field (and elsewhere), but I'd been content to take out my amateur anger on his ties with scissors and leave the drones to the professionals.

Which left Karyn.

If somehow the police suspected me of being a Sleeper, I needed to stay out of sight. I ducked into an alley that ran past the back of the neighborhood body salon, crouched behind a large metal recycler, and removed the old-fashioned letter from my pocket. There hadn't been a postal service for decades, so the mere feel of the letter in my hand brought back so many memories from my youth—Valentine cards from middle-school crushes, acceptances from colleges, bureaucratic form letters from my days working for the European Commission.

The sight of my mother's familiar handwriting, the kind of cursive no one uses anymore, produced a scrim of tears that momentarily blurred the first lines of the letter.

My dear daughter,

I don't have much time, so this will be short. I love you very much. Let me write that now in case I run out of time and space.

We tried my experiment, and it didn't work. The crystallization process, which would have created a homeostatic regrowth of the ice cap, didn't take. I think I know why, and Karyn has verified my calculations. But I don't have the right equipment to try again. I'm sending Karyn to you. She has all the information.

You just need to connect her with Benjamin. Only Benjamin can protect her.

Be aware that she thinks she is alive, that she is human. What a lovely bug in her software, what a special ghost in her machine.

I am sending Karyn to you. And I am heading in the other direction to give her more of a chance. I don't think I will get very far. You remember the legend of Inuit people putting their old ones on ice floes to die? It was more like assisted suicide. And so it will evidently be with me. But how glorious for a glaciologist to die on the ice, what little remains of it so close here to the pole.

I love you, dear Aurora. There, I was able to write it again after all. Be strong. On your shoulders rests so much. Give my love to your brothers and your precious sons. I will miss you all so terribly much.

Your mother

As I read her words, it was as if a giant fist was squeezing me tighter and tighter. By the end of the letter, I had to steady myself against the wall. I labored to breathe. Deprived of oxygen, the little flame inside me sputtered out. My mother: finally gone.

Her letter created a large heart-shaped gap inside me. And then, just as quickly, the anger rushed in to fill the void. In addition to a letter of love, my mother had sent me a walking, talking piece of unexploded ordnance. As long as Karyn remained with me, I would be a target.

And she would remain with me until I delivered her to Benjamin. Except that I had no idea how to get in touch with my baby brother. The last I looked, he was still the world's most wanted terrorist, in charge of the Movement, the largest secret army on the planet. He was without a doubt the most difficult person in the world to find.

My mother might as well have instructed me to deliver Karyn to the Abominable Snowman.

Babble

Welcome to our meeting space.

You have my bio—and the syllabus, such as it is. I've sent you all the class texts, my seven poems in English and French. I'm also including the seven original source poems.

During our time together, you can ask questions through the chat box.

Most of you have taken at least one of our courses, so you know the drill. As always, I'm not sure how much time we'll have here. I'm not sure how much material I can cover. I'm not sure of anything anymore. I do know, however, that if the light turns red, they know we're here, and we have to disconnect. Immediately.

As long as the light is green, we're safe.

To be honest, I'm not even sure why I agreed to teach this class. Commenting on one's own poetry is akin to a comic explaining a punch line or Sigmund Freud lying down on the couch to analyze himself. It's obviously a job for someone else. I once made my living in the classroom, explaining other people's words. I'm not altogether comfortable applying the same techniques to my own.

This is not meant to be a literary seminar. Rather, it's part of an attempt to make sense of our new reality. If I can help in this effort to explain the origins and purposes of our new common project, then I'm obligated to do so. Since my poems, these seven poems in particular, are inextricably bound up with that very project, I'll use them as convenient signposts for our trip.

Any questions?

No?

Okay, then let's begin.

When I was in my twenties, I watched helplessly as the world unraveled. I worked in Brussels, at the European Union, which seemed like such a solid edifice at the time. The member countries were still talking about expansion, building additions, creating new wings that would encompass the former Soviet Union, the western Balkans, even Turkey. That kind of conversation didn't last long. The builders fell to such squabbling that they tore the enterprise apart, one petty withdrawal after another. Forget about building additions. Our time was spent negotiating subtractions.

As you know, of course, the United Nations ultimately suffered the same fate—at the hands of those who attacked the concept of "one government" but in fact despised government of all kinds. China, Russia, the United States: they'd each progressed even further toward a common language only to split apart at the seams. You've probably read my father's magnum opus, *Splinterlands*, so you know the familiar arguments. I'm not telling you anything new.

To understand that destructive process, I devoted one of my earliest poems to a foundational myth: the Tower of Babel. I'm sure you have an image of the tower in your mind, like this one from a painting by Brueghel. It looks like a confection, doesn't it? A wedding cake, perhaps, or a giant cinnamon bun.

The biblical version of this story contains little information. After the flood, which swept iniquity from the world, the descendants of Noah's children—Ham, Shem, and Japheth—repopulated the land. Naturally, they spoke the same familial language. The progeny of one of those sons, having arrived at a suitable plain, decided to make a name for themselves. They baked bricks and mixed mortar. They built a great tower, which a jealous god saw as a challenge to his authority. Should they finish that building, the master architect of the universe decided, "nothing will be restrained from them, which they have imagined to do." So he cast a spell upon the builders.

From then on, Noah's descendants would not speak a common language. They suffered the fate that they most feared: to be scattered across the face of the earth. Ever since, we benighted humans have sorted through the pieces strewn on the floor to understand how they once formed a coherent whole.

As a young poet, I was transfixed by that moment when the builders abruptly changed their minds about what they were building. A shadow fell upon their efforts, and they shivered in bewilderment. A noise surrounded them, like the flapping of wings. But it was really the sound of their own voices. It was the sound of cacophony.

As I wrote in the final stanza of my poem "Babble,"

We couldn't see the tower as it was.

La tour, el torre, wieza, stolp, *and* torn.

We forgot our goal and gave up our tools,

and gazed out at the world as if reborn.

The Tower of Babel has had a disproportionately malign influence on our culture; it has rendered arrogant and treacherous the search for a common language, a common enterprise, anything in common. All joint ventures, built in the shadow of Babel, turn into follies to be abandoned before completion in favor of something new.

We all know, however, that new is not always better. As my irreligious mother used to say, born again just turns you back into a drooling baby.

With my own Babel poem, I began my cycle of reimagined epics. I combed through the world of poetry for forgotten classics into which I could breathe new life. It would be my attempt to recreate a common language, my modest project to repair the splintered world through song.

So you can understand why, when it came time to name our new effort several years ago, I was quick to make my suggestion. We should call it Babel.

"But you're dooming the venture with that single word!" someone objected. "A half-built tower. An angry god."

Oh no, I replied. It's time to reclaim the word, the story, the tradition. Our world has splintered; we have failed to lower the global thermostat. So isn't it time to go back to where the problem began? Isn't it time to pick up the tools and begin to rebuild? Through this joint work, we can at last construct a common language.

This time perhaps we'll ignore that jealous god. This time perhaps we will prove capable of raising our Babel to the very heavens.

This time we won't give up.

Chapter 3

Karyn was waiting for me inside the chop shop. Her new finger was slightly darker than the rest of her hand. She seemed a great deal more animated, as if she'd just knocked back a double espresso.

"You returned," she addressed me with a smile.

"I promised I would. Did you doubt me?"

She pursed her lips. "Perhaps I have abandonment issues."

I had no time to delve into AI psychology. "A drone strike just destroyed my apartment. Do you have any idea why?"

She was suddenly interested in her new finger. "It might have something to do with me."

"You could have warned me."

"I was not firing on all cylinders when I first saw you. Is that the right expression?"

I turned to the older model AI that ran the shop. "Can she be traced to here?"

"We are off the grid," the AI said proudly. "We offer absolute security to our exclusive clientele."

Of course. Chop shops were notorious for repurposing stolen goods. "And if the police are looking for me?"

"They were already here," the AI said, pointing at my wrist.

I'd forgotten my credit charge. I was obviously not cut out for undercover work. I would have made a lousy Sleeper. "What did you say? Did you tell them about—?"

"I said that you made a purchase and left after four minutes and 15 seconds. I didn't expect to see you again."

"Do you also have abandonment issues?" Karyn asked the AI.

"Thank you," I said, relieved. I'd somehow found the one safe space in South Brussels for us. "We'll just stay here until we can figure out who is after you, Karyn, and how we can track down my brother."

"But you can't stay here," the AI said.

"Come again?" I wasn't sure I'd heard correctly.

"You have to leave. It's the rules of the establishment."

"My apartment was just destroyed!" I exploded. "Some- one wants to kill us!"

"I'm sorry," the AI said. "It's the rules. The owner is very firm. You must leave within five minutes of complet- ing your final transaction. Or else my assistant will physi- cally remove you."

The assistant, now repaired, stood quietly at attention against the wall. Taller than its boss, with a snout and pointy erect ears, it was a metallic biped version of a guard dog. Its joints looked so rickety, however, that I would have wagered that it would topple over the second it tried to walk.

I put up my fists. I felt like a cornered child, and the words bubbled up from some repressed recess of my soul. "If you try to remove us, I will physically knock your block off. And your assistant's block as well!"

Karyn held up her hand. "Please, Aurora, let me see what I can do."

She turned toward the AI, and there ensued a few moments of silence.

"Okay," the AI finally said. "You can stay."

"What did you just do?" I whispered to Karyn, fearful of saying something that could inadvertently reverse the decision.

Karyn spoke at a normal volume. "We just had to discuss the possible exceptions to the rules. We can stay under Protocol 35, Section D."

"Thank god for Protocol 35, Section D," I breathed. I turned back to the AI. "Thank you for your hospitality."

"It is a pleasure to serve you both. Most of the time."

I sighed. "So, why didn't a drone hit us on the way over here?"

"Karyn has a very sophisticated scrambling technology," the AI replied.

"Then why was my apartment destroyed?"

The AI addressed Karyn. "You left your bag in the apartment."

"Yes, with a knife, my finger, a stuffed animal—"

"The finger," the AI interrupted. "Once it was outside her scramble zone, the finger could be traced."

"If we go back outside, will Karyn's scrambling technology keep us safe?" I asked.

"Now that they have one data point, they could locate us," Karyn admitted. "They have access to local surveillance cameras and satellite imagery."

"And who is they?"

Karyn looked troubled, and I worried that she would again start hitting herself. "I used to think that I was just a freelance welder with an artistic bent."

I eyed her skeptically. "A welder?"

"With your mother's help, I was able to recover some earlier memories. I discovered that I once worked for CRISPR. I imagine that's who's after us."

I should have guessed. CRISPR was a multinational corporation that had made its fortune with bioengineered drugs. Two years before, representatives of that business had "invited" me to Australia to talk about a research project of my father's, only releasing me when he gave them whatever they were looking for. Now, it seemed, I was again writhing at the center of its sticky web.

"What did you do for CRISPR?"

"I was a scout. I collected and relayed information. I was part of an attack on your mother's home."

"Arcadia?"

"I was just following orders. It was before. . . . I knew better."

"Why do they want to destroy you?"

"For one thing, I have all the information about our ice experiment."

"And why aren't you relaying it to your former employer?"

Karyn paused, as if making a complicated moral calculation. "CRISPR is bad."

"Because. . . ?"

"It wanted to kill my friends."

Even I could understand that this was an astonishing conclusion. If Karyn had "worked" for CRISPR, she'd probably been built by CRISPR. Which meant that she'd turned against her creators and sided with the "enemy." What coders call the "fealty algorithm" makes such betrayals at least theoretically impossible.

"So, what do you plan to do with this information?" I asked.

"Your mother suggested that I give it to your brother Benjamin."

"Do you have any idea where he is?"

She slapped her hand lightly against her forehead. Then, with an effort, she pressed her arm against her side. "Sorry, I'm trying to stop doing that."

"If we walk outside, we die. If we stay in here, we can play an endless guessing game about the location of my brother."

"There's someone I know who can help us." Karyn looked deep into my eyes. "Do you have a retinal implant?"

"I haven't used it in a couple weeks. I was getting error messages."

Karyn raised her hand near my eyes. "May I?"

I nodded.

I felt the softness of her palm against my eye socket. There was no warmth. But the gentleness of her touch nevertheless seemed human.

"You just needed to update the operating system," Karyn said. "It works now."

I blinked three times. My inbox was overflowing. I saw several messages from my children. They didn't know anything about what had happened to their grandmother or their grandfather. Now I had to figure out what to tell them about Karyn and our former apartment. As soon as I had a moment, I'd DM them both to arrange a time to talk.

"Shall we go?" Karyn asked.

"Where?"

"To Arcadia."

"What's in Arcadia?"

"Some smart friends."

My mother had lived in Arcadia for nearly thirty years— before she set off on her suicide mission to the Arctic. I knew very little about the place. I'd visited only once, and my mother didn't talk much about her home when she visited me in Brussels. Located in what had once been the state of Vermont, Arcadia was fully self-sustainable, not to mention heavily armed because of the paramilitaries that were a constant threat to its existence.

"Are they smarter than you?"

"I'm smarter than it," Karyn said, pointing back at the obediently silent AI. "And I'm smarter than you. But I am not smarter than they are."

"I'll try not to take offense."

I thought: Just try to parse a John Ashbery poem or, better yet, write one of your own. I then comforted myself by imagining that Karyn was referring to a very specific kind of task-oriented intelligence. After all, my poetic expertise notwithstanding, I couldn't figure out how to get out of this chop shop without dying in a drone strike. Nor could I locate my brother Benjamin. Perhaps she was right and these "smart friends" in Arcadia could.

"Are you ready to go?" Karyn asked.

"They can't track us in VR space?"

"If you were alone, they could track you because you have a previous generation of retinal implant. But we will hold hands. By yoking, we can travel together. That way, I can take you through the dark web."

"Will this . . . yoking hurt?"

"Not in the least."

Still anxious, I reached for her hand and readied myself to make the jump.

When I was growing up, virtual reality was rudimentary. You could only travel to virtual worlds of varying degrees of verisimilitude. Navigating them required elaborate gear and a strong stomach.

In the 2020s, the COVID-19 pandemic spurred the invention of an entirely different kind of augmented reality. Thanks to the new technology, those who were sheltering in place could travel virtually to real places and interact with the people there in real time. Initially, only the wealthy could afford trips to the first Vi-Fi-enabled destinations: Manhattan, the Grand Canyon, Mt. Kilimanjaro. As the infrastructure spread, the prices went down and the locations multiplied. Eventually you could travel practically anywhere in the world.

Vi-Fi has been a game changer, contributing to the further contraction of time and space and keeping the world connected even as so many global institutions disappeared. When air travel became precipitously expensive, VR allowed for nearly carbon-free globe-trotting. Today, you can visit war zones, if disaster tourism is your thing, and pandemic hotspots to say goodbye to a friend or family member. VR allows paraplegics to run in actual marathons. You can even fool yourself into thinking that you're playing first violin with the Berlin Philharmonic or having sex with your long-distance fiancé. In the deluxe versions, you can actually taste the *kaiseki* meal in your *ryokan* in Kyoto. In other words, you can easily forget that you're not really there.

But not me. I can never let myself "go with the flow." I just don't relish the sensation of being disembodied. I realize that, according to the norms of the time, I'm exhibiting an unconscious "body privilege." And I have no doubt that, as my body more frequently betrays me, I'll inevitably do what everyone of a certain age does these days: turn to VR to escape the clutches of entropy.

Although I've never been a fan of VR—and I might even be a neo-Luddite, as my husband insists—I'm not an Abstinent. I don't believe, like the followers of William the Abstinent, that VR has infected humanity at all levels, including the molecular one. I don't wear one of the cult's special headbands to protect my brain from the "virus of Vi-Fi." Quite the contrary: I've made my accommodations over the years, even attending VR conferences and interacting with colleagues in VR faculty meetings. To talk to my children when they're at school I've had to meet them in exotic locales of their choosing—a nook in Timbuktu or a cranny in Andalusia—anywhere wired with Vi-Fi, which now has almost universal reach.

There's definitely a generational divide. My children, fully immersed in the VR world, are comfortable interacting with all the shadowy avatars that populate it. They're always talking to people I don't see and playing games with friends I never meet. They ridicule me for favoring flatland over their multidimensional world. I tell them that they reside in a realm of ghosts.

Grasping Karyn's soft hand, I prepared myself mentally to leave what the younger generation so graphically calls meatspace and enter that land of shadows.

Chapter 4

We found ourselves stuck in VR quarantine: a white room where we could do nothing other than stand and wait. I knew this would happen the moment Karyn suggested we visit Arcadia. On my one previous virtual visit to the compound, even with my mother vouching for me, I'd spent two hours in this waiting room—just like the old days when security risks were plucked from arrival queues at airports. In this VR limbo, I was subjected to endless questions and a battery of unseen tests to make sure that my avatar and I were identical and that the former harbored no malicious viruses.

Arcadia couldn't be too careful. They'd had several very unpleasant experiences with attempted infiltration, so I knew not to take it personally.

Arcadia was armed and well-protected for a reason. What had once been the United States was now a low-intensity war zone. The government, such as it was, maintained control over an archipelago of military bases and a well-armed capital in Kansas City. Several sub-state entities like Northern California had managed to survive relatively intact. The rest of the land, including this patch of territory hard up against the former border with Quebec, shifted hands constantly from one paramilitary force to another. White supremacists had even tried to create a New Albion across Vermont, New Hampshire, and Maine, and remnants of those forces continued to pursue this dream. Arcadia was a candle in the darkness. Its state-of-the-art arsenal served as a shield to prevent the flame from sputtering out.

I'd learned from Karyn that Arcadia had recently come under a more sustained attack from CRISPR. She'd been part of this attempted breach until she was captured and "turned." I was a little hazy about the reasons for CRISPR's attack. I couldn't really understand why such a powerful corporation would be interested in such a marginal community, especially since I'd never taken Arcadia very seriously myself. I couldn't help seeing it as an anachronistic back-to-the-earth movement crossed with a survivalist compound: organic agriculture, solar energy, self-sufficiency, and semi-automatics. In the anarchy of an unraveled America, Arcadia had become the equivalent of a walled city-state from the Middle Ages.

A young woman with a pixie haircut in the homespun dress of another century finally ushered us out of the quarantine room.

"Hello, Lizzie, I'm very happy to see you again," Karyn said, adding in an aside to me, "Lizzie interrogated me when I first came to Arcadia. She was very nice."

"Welcome back, Karyn," Lizzie said warmly in the clipped Yankee accent of someone born in the community. She looked at me approvingly. "I like your avatar. She has a big following around here."

It took a moment for me to understand her reference. Then I remembered that I'd chosen an image of the poet Emily Dickinson, in her twenties with a mysterious half-smile on her lips, as my default profile. "I'm so glad to hear that her poetry is still popular."

"Not so much her poetry as her quiet nonconformity." Blushing, Lizzie quickly changed the subject. "Speaking of heroes, we miss your mother very much, Aurora. She was a great woman." Lizzie caught herself. "*Is* a great woman. She'll always be in our hearts and in our memories."

I felt tears welling up and wondered whether they would be visible on my avatar's face. "I'm here because of her," I said, trying to will the tears back into their ducts.

"You've come at a rather awkward time," Lizzie said, escorting us down a corridor to the threshold of a large room. "Perhaps Zoltan can explain."

She pushed open the door to reveal a young man with platinum hair seated by himself in a large room. He was staring at a bank of computer screens through metal-frame glasses of the sort I hadn't seen in years, not since retinal implants had rendered them unnecessary. Like Lizzie's dress, they reminded me yet again of Arcadia's special place in the space–time fabric: simultaneously old-fashioned and super-modern.

Zoltan swiveled a quarter turn to greet us. "You probably don't remember me, Aurora," he said in a soft, sibilant voice. "I was only twelve years old when you visited your mother. I'm now one of the cochairs here, along with Lizzie. I'll be debriefing you."

Lizzie gestured for me to enter the room before continuing with Karyn down the corridor.

"This is our office," Zoltan said, taking in the room with a proud sweep of his hand. Then he sighed. "But it increasingly feels like a compound. A compound within a compound."

"Why are you debriefing us separately?"

"I want to tell you some things that I don't want Karyn to hear. I can't be entirely certain of her loyalties."

I bristled. "She went with my mother to the Arctic. And now she's being targeted by CRISPR. Those seem like pretty good bona fides to me."

"Your mother's ice experiment didn't succeed, did it?"

"No, it didn't." In a flash, I saw where he was heading. "And CRISPR didn't succeed in destroying her either."

"Precisely."

"If you had questions about her loyalty, why did you let us out of quarantine?"

Zoltan tilted a computer screen so that I could see it. "Because of this."

Row after row of code was scrolling down the screen. "I don't understand."

"Each line is a separate cyberattack," Zoltan explained. "One hundred and sixty-three in the last ten minutes alone. CRISPR is trying to take over our systems. If we don't do something soon, they'll breach our firewall."

"I hope you're not expecting us to help."

"You already have. I'm using Karyn as bait. To see whether she tries to contact anyone while she's here. Or if anyone tries to reach out to her."

"You think she's still working for CRISPR. That she's a spy."

"Or perhaps she's a spy for someone inside Arcadia. Maybe she's only working for herself. What we're doing is standard operating procedure in case of the singularity."

"Wait, what do you mean, someone inside Arcadia?"

Zoltan bit his lip. "As Lizzie said, you've come at a rather awkward moment here in this community."

I knew next to nothing about life inside Arcadia. I remembered a few references my mother had made to a schism nearly three decades past. I'd assumed that unanimity had reigned since. Not that I was interested: I'd come to get only one piece of information.

"Well, it's an awkward time for me as well." I repeated what I'd said in the quarantine room about the surprise appearance of Karyn, the letter from my mother, the destruction of my apartment. "My body is stuck in a chop shop in South Brussels for the foreseeable future. I have a target on my back, thanks to Karyn and CRISPR's desire to destroy what remains of my mother's research."

Zoltan was now pacing the room. I wanted to grab him by the shoulders and force him to stand still, but my hands would have just passed right through him.

"If this were a conventional chess game, the play would be straightforward." His eyes were half-closed as he addressed the ceiling. "Karyn is a pawn that your mother sacrificed in her attempt to checkmate CRISPR in the Arctic. Or she's a pawn that we're protecting to help Arcadia. In the worst-case scenario, she's a pawn on the other team that CRISPR steadily advances until she makes it behind our defenses, at which point she becomes a far more powerful and destructive queen."

"That doesn't sound straightforward at all, not if she can be any one of three different pawns."

His eyes refocused on me. "I said *if* this were a conventional chess game. I don't think it is. If Karyn were a spy, I don't think she'd advance down the board in plain view. So, here's my hypothesis: Karyn is not a pawn or a would-be queen. She's a piece that has never been seen on the chessboard. She's a piece that moves by itself. That doesn't need a guiding hand."

"She's an AI," I said, trying to understand the drift of Zoltan's thinking. "She's an AI who doesn't think she's an AI."

"Precisely. She's the singularity."

"She's certainly singular."

Zoltan was growing excited, and his eyes glistened behind his glasses. "No, no, the *singularity*. She is the first example of artificial consciousness. She doesn't just have a brain, she has a mind. It's why she doesn't think she's an AI. She doesn't think she's artificial at all."

"But my mother wrote that this belief of hers is a software error."

"Exactly! That's what consciousness is!" Zoltan was punctuating his points with finger jabs. "Consciousness is a bug. At some point in our evolutionary development, a bug in our genetic software occurred and—bam!—one of our ancestors became conscious. It is the same way that life appeared magically in the primordial soup. And now Karyn is the latest cosmic magic trick."

"She's . . . human?"

Zoltan's hands fluttered in the air as if he were trying to rearrange the sentences as they left his mouth. "No, no, no. A conscious dolphin isn't a human. Karyn's better than a human. You've seen her in action."

"She was running low on power. She just seemed tired to me."

Zoltan resumed pacing and talking to the ceiling. "This is what I'm thinking. She was part of the first wave that CRISPR sent to test our defenses. The drones, the AIs: they were all set to self-destruct after sending back the information they gathered. But Karyn didn't self-destruct. I think that's when she became conscious. Up to that point, she was just another piece of metal. Smart metal maybe, but just a robot. I don't know whether it was something we did or something that went wrong with her self-destruct mechanism. Whatever it was, it functioned like the word of God. Or a lightning bolt."

Now, I could see where Zoltan was heading. "She's not a spy then. And you think that CRISPR's aware of what she is."

"Yes."

"Why aren't they just trying to capture her?"

"I'm guessing that's not so easy. Karyn is potentially very dangerous. And it's not just the contents of her memory. It's the full range of her capabilities. She's unboxed."

"How could Karyn be dangerous? The only person she could harm is herself when she hits her forehead."

"But what if she decides to create a robot army to take over the world?"

I glared at him. "Don't we have more immediate threats to worry about?"

"She is still an infant, you know, maybe a year old. Infants aren't aware of themselves. We're shaped through our interactions with our environment. Karyn the toddler will be a great deal different from Karyn the infant. Karyn the angry child could throw a very dangerous tantrum."

"She's not a child. And wouldn't her programmers have included some . . . some . . ."

"Fail-safes. Yes, but soon they may not apply. Do your children still obey your commandments?"

"How will we know if she's with us or against us?"

Zoltan held out his hands, palms up. "Common sense."

"You're relying on my common sense?"

"Not your common sense. *Her* common sense. If she looks at the world solely through logic, she might well decide that humans are better off as brains floating in vats and that she's a better steward of the world than we are."

"I'd be inclined to agree with her."

Zoltan pushed his glasses up the bridge of his nose, and I was suddenly reminded of everything I disliked about wearing glasses as a child—that pinch at my nose, that rubbing behind my ears, that blurring of the world at the edges. Retinal implants came with an upgrade to 20/20 vision. Technology had some benefits. Maybe Karyn was just the upgrade humanity needed to see clearly at this particularly fraught moment.

"Or," Zoltan continued, "she might decide that it's better to preserve the 1 percent and let the 99 percent disappear beneath the waves, that climate change is good for the planet, that a few rich immortals are an improvement over billions of wasteful mortals. She might decide that CRISPR's strategy is the only way to save the planet."

I'd also heard the rumors that CRISPR had developed an immortality drug and had built enclaves where its rich clientele could live far from the rising tides. It was the same survivalist fantasy that had gripped the techno-elite for decades. I'd always figured it was more of an aspiration than an actual deliverable.

"But wouldn't Karyn's version of common sense be different from ours?"

Zoltan wasn't listening. "If I'd figured all this out before, I'd never have sent her off with your mother to the Arctic. She's far too valuable. You've got to do everything in your power to protect her."

"Me? I'm just a poet!"

At that moment, Lizzie reappeared at the threshold. "I'm sorry to interrupt. I just wanted to let you know that we ran the tests. Karyn didn't contact anyone inside or outside of Arcadia."

"Excellent," Zoltan said. "Set her up at the auxiliary hub and let's see if she can help us with these cyberattacks. As for you, Aurora, let's get you together with Benjamin, as your mother suggested in her letter to you. Benjamin will understand the stakes."

"I have no idea how to get in touch with him."

"We don't either. But there is someone who does, someone who holds you in the highest regard."

Chapter 5

I'd met Emmanuel Puig only once. He'd paid me a VR visit in South Brussels to solicit permission to publish my mother's manuscript, something she'd put together before heading off to the Arctic on her quixotic mission. I'd skimmed the text, focusing on the sections that mentioned me, and then forwarded it to Puig as my mother had requested.

He didn't need my permission since my mother had already granted that. It turned out what he really wanted was to encourage me to write something of my own. I brushed him off. I was busy preparing for a New Year's Eve party. I had my classes to teach, my sociological research to conduct, the latest poem to laboriously unfurl from my subconscious. I had nothing to offer him, so I made no promises. He misinterpreted my refusal as thoughtful consideration and has been pestering me for a manuscript ever since.

Puig is an eccentric character. He knows more about my family than I do. He's been busy annotating an updated version of my father's famous *Splinterlands* thesis that he completed just before he died. And now he's also editing my mother's manuscript as a kind of sequel. To fact-check those, Puig had been in touch not only with Gordon, my financier brother in Ningxia, but also with the elusive Benjamin, my youngest brother. If I'd read my mother's manuscript more carefully I would have known that.

Zoltan, who updated me on Puig's latest projects, was convinced that the esteemed professor could put me in touch with Benjamin.

"I traveled here with Karyn," I reminded Zoltan. "We're holding hands back in South Brussels. Don't I need to travel with her?"

"As long as you're still holding hands back there, you're still yoked. So you don't need to travel together. I can show you how to add a visit to Buenos Aires to your dark web itinerary."

"What if Puig doesn't want to meet?"

"Trust me," Zoltan said. "He'll drop everything to see you."

With Zoltan's help, I jumped virtually to Buenos Aires, where Puig runs an institute devoted to geo-paleontology, the discipline that my father created to study the rise and fall of such dinosaurs as the Soviet Union and the European Union. Even though he was presiding over an important academic conference, Puig instantly agreed to meet.

We arranged a rendezvous by the statue of Rodin's *Thinker* in the Plaza del Congreso, the park that faces what had been the Argentine Congress before Patagonia seceded and the country fell apart. Buenos Aires is now a mini-state and the congressional building serves as its seat of government.

"Aurora!" he cried out on spotting me next to the statue. "It is so good to see you again! You and Emily Dickinson!"

Puig is tall and so thin he's practically two-dimensional. He has ink-black hair and a neatly trimmed goatee. When he's thinking, he furrows his brow and juts out his bottom lip, which makes him look like a child on the verge of a tantrum. Single-minded and pitiless, he's exactly the kind of academic that governments love to hire to implement unpopular policies. To obscure these otherwise unattractive traits, much as he's grown a goatee to conceal his weak chin, Puig affects great enthusiasm and appends exclamation points to the end of nearly every sentence.

"Thank you for seeing me on such short notice," I said.

"I do anything to meet with you!" he exclaimed. "Always!"

We began to circle the fountains in the park, which were edged by rose beds alive with colorful butterflies. It was a sunny spring day, and many couples were walking hand in hand. A busker sat on a folding chair playing tango music on an accordion. Avatars, too, were out in force. A grey hooded figure talked with an obviously delighted young woman. A troop of flickering shadows were playing tag with two copiously sweating boys. It felt festive, as if Buenos Aires weren't besieged like Arcadia or South Brussels.

I was suddenly distracted by a movement at the corner of my vision—a little girl running up and planting herself in front of me.

"Please help me, Aurora!" she pleaded.

"I'm sorry, do I know you?"

"I'm being chased," she said breathlessly. "I need your help!"

I felt my heartbeat quicken. "Chased by whom?"

"The White Tigers! They're right behind me!"

I looked around but didn't see anyone in pursuit. Emmanuel was frowning.

"I don't see anyone," I said.

"Please, please follow the link on your screen," the girl implored.

In bright yellow letters, PLEASE HELP! floated across my line of sight.

"Please help me, Aurora!" the girl said again, holding out her hands.

I was moved by her tear-streaked face, the sobs wracking her tiny frame. As I reached out to grasp her hands, Emmanuel intervened.

"I must apologize," he said, his hand sweeping away the next sentence that appeared in the air between us: YOU CAN HELP DEFEAT GLOBAL TERRORISM. "These NGO phishers are becoming so intrusive."

The girl disappeared. I struggled to catch my breath.

"She's not real," he reassured me. "I have just changed the settings for our meeting: no more interruptions, I promise. Now, what can I do for you, my dear?"

I swallowed hard. Importuning him as I was, I couldn't help but feel like that little girl. "I have a favor to ask of you," I began.

He lit up. "You have a manuscript for me! I will edit! I will publish!"

"No, I don't have a manuscript for you."

"But you will? You promised!"

"I didn't promise."

"You are a writer, Aurora. It is in your blood. You must write!"

"First I need to see my brother."

"You mean Gordon? Perhaps he will finance a sabbatical for you to write?"

I rolled my eyes. "I'd never ask Gordon to do that. I'm already in debt to him."

"I see." Emmanuel Puig looked down. "You want to see your other brother."

"You're the only person I know who has any contact with Benjamin."

"He is indeed a secretive man."

"I need his help."

He furrowed his brow and jutted his lip. "I think I smell a story."

I had a sudden urge to send Emmanuel Puig to a corner of the park for a time out. "If you give me his contact information," I said slowly, "then I will write something for you."

"It will be such an honor!" Puig clapped his hands. Then, turning sober, he said, "Your mother. Have you heard any words from her?"

I shook my head, unwilling to give away any clues.

"I am so sorry, Aurora! Her manuscript will be her testament."

"I know that it's in good hands," I said, without meaning it. "Now, can you give me Benjamin's address?"

"I must leave a message at a safe location with your co-ordinates. And then he will contact you. Or. . ."

"Or?"

"Or he won't. Your brother is rather selective."

I lost my temper. "He damn well better contact me! This is a matter of life or death!"

"I will be sure to convey the urgency of your request."

"Please do." I took several deep breaths. I was unaccustomed to making threats. "If I don't see my brother, there will be no manuscript."

Puig suddenly looked frantic.

"But I'm sure that you will be at your most persuasive," I reassured him. "After all, your trilogy depends on it."

Europa

Metamorphosis is at the heart of myth, and myth is at the center of civilization. We all want to know how water becomes steam, how the caterpillar becomes a butterfly, how the vast lifeless oceans became the cradle of life. And now, we are desperate to understand how a matrix of silicon can fool us into thinking that it's human.

How to get from A to B? That's such a pedestrian question. We want to know how A *becomes* B.

You, meanwhile, want to know how we created our movement, how nothing became something. That's why we're here. You and I are part of this something, this *becoming*. But what are we becoming?

I was introduced to Ovid's *Metamorphoses* at university. The Roman poet was a near contemporary of Jesus, another great example of transformation, of God becoming man, of Word becoming flesh and dwelling among us. In the *Metamorphoses*, everyone is in the process of becoming, none more so than the otherwise unchanging gods. Jupiter, for instance, can't sit still because of a lust he cannot master, so he turns himself into a succession of avatars—a swan, a shower of gold—to get by the defenses of young women. To seduce the beautiful maiden Europa, he even takes the form of a lowly bull.

However much I was entranced by Ovid, I was furious when I read his description of Jupiter's bovine plan to seize Europa. This was how Europe was conceived? Through rape? It was an instructive lesson. In my poem dedicated to Europa I later wrote:

Europe, too, was born of sin,
delivered through clench and pain.
After war and rape and so much blood,
civilization crawled from the mud.

When I was in my twenties, after finishing my degree in sociology, I moved to Brussels to take a position at the European Commission. I don't really know why I did this. I'd always wanted to be a poet, not a bureaucrat. But my father, a political scientist, had been enamored of the European project. Naturally, I wanted his approval. I also thought I could make a difference. In comparison to saving Europe, poetry seemed a paper project, so I put those hopes on hold.

We failed. Europe fell apart like a precious glass bowl dropped on the hard, stone floor.

Why did the European Union fall apart? Thank you for the question, @emgoldman2050.

Perhaps the flaws had been sealed in the glass from the beginning, as Europe fractured along predictable fault lines. Don't listen to the populists or the literary theorists: it's much simpler to deconstruct than to construct. Handled with greater care, the bowl could have survived many more decades. Unlike curators, though, politicians don't wear velvet gloves. And the ones we elected in the teens and twenties were like bulls in the proverbial china shop. Everything they touched turned to shards.

My parents named me Aurora because they were optimists. Aurora, after all, means "dawn," and they felt they were at the dawn of a new era. It's been my great misfortune, however, to be present at the end: of the EU, of the international community, possibly of the world as we know it.

On the eve of the European Union's disintegration, I wrote my poem "Europa" as a warning: don't listen to the seductions of the powerful even if they promise you a principality. But I should have remembered my Greek mythology. No one listens to Cassandra.

Too late to warn:
Don't mount the bull.
Don't wade out to sea.
Don't become an abductee.

As Europe shattered around me and my job became redundant, I could have/should have/would have become a full-time poet. But as a parent, I felt I had to be practical. Necessity is not the mother of invention. It is the mother of accommodation. It is the mother of two children. Following my Ph.D. rather than my passion, I took an academic post in my chosen field of sociology.

I was angry in those days. Very, very angry. And this was even before my husband began to philander. I was angry because I'd been transformed into something I didn't like—a nagging mother, an unhappy wife, a distant daughter. A non-poet.

In Ovid, women metamorphize to escape becoming the playthings of the gods. Daphne becomes a Laurel tree, Cornix a crow, Syrinx a water reed.

Eventually I, too, would metamorphize. But not for me the role of Jupiter's victim. I would choose a different avatar altogether.

As a matador, I would grab the bull by the horns.

Chapter 6

When I returned to Arcadia, I thought I'd mistakenly leaped into a barroom brawl. A siren was going off. The office where I'd talked with Zoltan was full of shouting people, and he was in front of his computer screens frantically swiping through maps pulsing with dots of differing intensities.

No one paid any attention to me.

"What's wrong?" I asked a tall woman in a turquoise sari. She waved me off as if I were a gnat buzzing in her ear.

Without thinking, I tried to tap someone on the shoulder. It was like trying to embrace a hologram. Frustrated, I took a position just behind Zoltan so that I could watch what he was doing.

"I can't find her," he was saying. "I can't find either of them."

A gruff man with a full beard and a French-Canadian accent was also looking at the screens. He spoke quietly into Zoltan's ear. "We can't access the VR room. Even if we could find them, we can't go after them."

Zoltan closed his eyes and leaned back. "I should have anticipated. . . I should have seen more moves ahead."

"You couldn't have known," the bearded man said. "She fooled everyone. I'm her father and she fooled me."

Zoltan took off his glasses and stared at them suspiciously as if they'd betrayed him. "We keep dividing into factions. Is it some natural law of human organization?"

"There's no one in here who has retinal implants?" the bearded man asked. "Not even one of the recent Captures?"

"No, Bertrand, there's nobody. The community made that decision before I was even born. No retinal implants. Too risky." Zoltan groaned. "I feel sick."

"Are you looking for me?" I asked. "Because I'm right here, Zoltan."

Zoltan swiveled in his chair. He squinted to focus on me with his watery eyes. "Aurora? You're back?"

"What's going on?" I asked.

"There's been a complication."

"Who's this?" Bertrand was now looking at me. "Is this the other one? The one who came with her?"

Zoltan nodded.

"Do you know where your friend is?" Bertrand asked me. "The AI?"

I looked at Zoltan. "Where's Karyn?"

He passed a hand over his eyes before restoring his glasses. "I thought I could use her to flush them out. I didn't expect that they would—"

"Who is *they*?" I asked.

He took a breath. "There's a faction here that wants to compromise with CRISPR."

"How is that even possible?" I demanded.

"We don't have time for this," Bertrand said, pointing at the screen. "We have to find them."

"We've been working on shoring up the defenses," Zoltan told me. "Karyn was helping us with a few important fixes and then—"

"My daughter took her," Bertrand interrupted. "She locked herself in the VR room and jumped somewhere in the world with this Karyn."

"Your daughter?"

"My daughter Lizzie."

I turned on Zoltan in fury. "I brought Karyn here because you were supposed to be smart and this was supposed to be safe!"

Zoltan looked like he was going to cry. "I thought that the one person Karyn was safe with was Lizzie. Lizzie! She's like a sister to me. Then I . . . Then after you left for Buenos Aires I got the DM from her. She said that this was the only way to save Arcadia. And she'll use Karyn to negotiate a deal to . . . I don't know. It's crazy. As if CRISPR would honor any deal."

I heard an internal ping. A notification in the upper right corner of my visual pane indicated an incoming DM from Emmanuel Puig. The message consisted only of a time—16:00 (GMT +4)—followed by a string of numbers.

"I need to go," I said. "I need to meet my brother."

"You're yoked," Zoltan said, nostrils flaring as if catching a whiff of a new scent in the room.

"If I miss this meeting with Benjamin, he won't trust me to show up a second time. I'm about to blow the one chance I have to . . ."

"You're yoked," Zoltan repeated. "And I don't think Lizzie knows that you can follow them."

"Who cares what she knows!" I said angrily. "How do I get out of here? I need to meet my brother in exactly 50 minutes."

"You'll have to find Karyn. In fact, you're the only one who can."

"Look, I don't know anything about this VR nonsense. I can't go on a search-and-rescue mission."

Bertrand interjected, "If my daughter gives away Karyn, we are through. Arcadia is done."

"I don't care about Arcadia!" I screamed.

The room went quiet, and now everyone was looking at me.

"I mean," I backpedaled, "what I mean is . . ."

"If CRISPR gets Karyn, they'll be able to trace you both back to wherever you are in South Brussels," Zoltan pointed out.

"Which means that you'll be done too," Bertrand said gently.

I took a moment to swallow my anger. "Okay, just tell me what to do."

"We need to hurry." Zoltan's voice had gained a sudden confidence. "Everyone out of the room!"

Bertrand was the last to leave. At the threshold, he turned back to me. "Your mother would have been very proud of you right now, Aurora."

Chapter 7

When my mother sent her parents their first computer, they didn't bother to take it out of the box. It sat in a corner of the bedroom where I slept during our visits to Chapel Hill. When my grandfather died, my mother tried to persuade the grieving widow to move in with us in Washington. My grandmother refused. She didn't want to leave her friends, her garden, her rocking chair on the front porch. The compromise: nightly video chats. But that meant opening up what my grandmother called "that Pandora's box upstairs."

My mother was too busy with her work, and my father had no patience for such things. So they flew me down to North Carolina to set everything up and cajole the poor old woman into using it. She'd swatted away the offers of neighbors. Surely, she'd give in to a persistent little girl.

I was nine years old at the time—precocious, self-important—and I was offended as only a preteen can be by how little my grandmother understood about the virtual world. Everything I took for granted, from wireless connections to the relationship between software and hardware, was like a foreign language for her. She refused even to own a cell phone and clung irrationally to a landline. During her career as an elementary school teacher, she'd started out with overhead projectors and never advanced much further than that. As I discovered when I set up her computer in the downstairs den, she even had difficulties navigating the computer interface with the mouse. It didn't make intuitive sense to her that moving the mouse in one direction corresponded to a similar trajectory on the screen. As I guided the mouse around its trackpad, I felt smart, worldly, and frankly superior to my grandmother, who knew far more about the world than I did.

And now, a few years past fifty years old, I would experience a similar humbling at the hands of Zoltan, who was half my age. He was grounded, without retinal implants or access to Arcadia's VR room, yet he was determined to prepare me for my next journey. I'd made the mistake of telling him about the NGO phisher in Buenos Aires, which revealed me to be the VR rookie I was. Even though I protested that I knew all this, he proceeded to give me a condensed tutorial on how to manipulate the virtual world—look down left for the main menu, blink twice for settings and three times for the inbox, shake my head to swipe through screens. He then instructed me on advanced commands, of which I was entirely ignorant. All that head twitching, which made virtual travelers look as if they were keeping beat to an internal soundtrack, gave me a headache.

"I only have forty minutes before my meeting with Benjamin," I reminded him.

"You'll have one chance," Zoltan said. "If you blow it, it's game over."

"You make it sound like a video game."

"I wish it were. In video games, you get multiple lives. Here, you have just one, and it might already be too late."

"Then let's go already!"

Finally, after another ten agonizing minutes of instruction, Zoltan set me up to jump.

Even though Karyn and I were yoked, it was no easy task to track her down. Lizzie and her conspirators had taken pains to cover their virtual footsteps. With Zoltan guiding me by DM, I searched for Karyn's trajectory, which was like picking out an unfamiliar constellation from the night sky. It took several precious minutes tracing the wrong shapes before I finally found her trail and copied her coordinates as Zoltan had shown me how to do. I had less than thirty minutes to get in and out with what I needed.

I jumped.

And landed in the middle of a hot scrum. Bodies, real and virtual, gyrated all around me.

"Welcome, my lovely," someone purred in my ear.

"Over here," cried someone else. "I totally want to do Emily Dickinson!"

I must have somehow dropped a number when inputting the coordinates. Dazzled by the loud music and swirling colors, I closed my eyes and concentrated on copying and pasting correctly.

The music disappeared. With intense relief, I found myself standing on a cliff overlooking a city bathed in late afternoon sunlight. Beyond its imposing sea walls, a vast ocean sparkled. My screen flashed the name of my location, the very same place I'd been taken two years before for a "friendly interview" about my father and his intentions.

Darwin, Northern Territories. The corporate headquarters of CRISPR.

Two people were having a conversation on the grassy verge. One of them was a stick figure, the most basic avatar for an anonymous lurker. She had a triangle for a face, another triangle for a dress, long zigzags for hair, and a half-moon smile. The other was an enormous man wearing a striped swimsuit. He looked like a beach ball on legs. Karyn, the abductee, stood stiffly off to the side. They all turned in surprise at my sudden appearance.

"How did you find us?" the stick figure asked. I recognized Lizzie's Yankee accent.

"What a lovely surprise!" The man had a resonant baritone. "A nineteenth-century poet."

"It's Aurora, Rachel's daughter," Lizzie said, her eyebrows tenting angrily and her charcoal eyes blazing. "Go away. We're almost finished here."

"This is a mistake, Lizzie." I was following Zoltan's script. "They can't be trusted."

"We've always honored our agreements with your family, Aurora," the man said. "I am more than a little disappointed. Did we not return you to South Brussels and your loving family?"

I didn't like the emphasis he put on "loving." I looked more closely at the man. Yes, he was one of the CRISPR representatives who'd "interviewed" me. I remembered a clinical setting, real fruit that I refused to eat, and pointed questions that I tried not to answer.

"This has nothing to do with you," Lizzie said. "This is about Arcadia. This is about *saving* Arcadia."

"If you want to save Arcadia, you'll let Karyn go. And you'll come back and negotiate with the right person: Zoltan."

"My dear," the fat man said. "CRISPR is the future. Lizzie is a visionary. And Arcadia really has no choice."

"There's always a choice," I said, without actually believing that myself.

"You can't understand," Lizzie said dismissively. "Zoltan wants to fight a war that he can't win. I'm negotiating a peace deal."

"And sacrificing Karyn."

"I'm sorry, Aurora, but it's not a sacrifice. Karyn is not a human. She's basically a highly capable drone."

Karyn cleared her throat. "I beg to differ."

"What good is Karyn's avatar to you?" I asked the fat man.

"Just a will-o'-the-wisp," he said, amiably. "But once Lizzie hands her over, we can find out where she is. Where you *both* are."

"And send out a swarm of drones to destroy us just like you destroyed my apartment."

"I apologize for that," the man said. "One of my assistants has an itchy finger. It won't happen again. Karyn is too valuable to destroy. And you, too, of course."

I turned to Lizzie. "I can't persuade you?"

Lizzie ignored me and addressed the man. "You'll keep our governing structure in place? And you won't punish anyone, including Zoltan?"

"We are not in the punishment business," the man assured her.

I took a step toward the trio. "Look, I don't need to witness your negotiations. If I can't persuade you, Lizzie, I'll just go."

"Good," the stick figure said.

The man smiled. "I'm always delighted to see you, Aurora. Please give my best to your brothers."

"I'll just say goodbye to my friend." I took another step, but this time toward Karyn.

"Keep it short," the stick figure said.

The fat man looked suddenly stricken. He lunged at me. "No, wait, don't let her—"

It was too late.

I easily evaded both his outstretched hands and Lizzie's flailing stick arms. I reached out to Karyn and grasped a ghostly finger. Perhaps it was just my imagination but I thought I experienced the slightest tingle on my tongue, like what I'd once felt licking a battery on a schoolyard dare. As soon as we were virtually in touch, it took less than a second for Zoltan's program to kick in, and then I could blink our way to the relative safety of South Brussels.

Chapter 8

Back in the chop shop, the AI was still behind the counter.

"Can I help you?" it asked.

"Oh, for Christ's sake," I said. "We've been standing here all along. Don't you recognize us?"

"You don't have to be rude," it said. "And the offer still stands: can I help you with something?"

I saw that the doglike assistant had again fallen over and was now slumped like a gunshot victim against a stack of circuit boards, its muzzle pressed against its chest. A gurgling sound issued from its torso.

"You could probably help your assistant," I pointed out.

"It's a temperamental model," the AI replied smoothly. "I'm printing a new BTP3490002. It should do the trick."

"Perhaps I could take a look at some point," Karyn offered.

"That would be a great help," the AI said.

I checked my retinal display. "We only have five minutes before our meeting. We have to get back on the road."

"The road?" the AI said.

"A figure of speech," I explained.

Karyn, meanwhile, was running her hands over her body, starting with her face, as if taking inventory. "Thank you for rescuing me."

"Don't mention it. Can we go now?"

"But you shouldn't have." She touched her toes.

"Really, it was not a—"

"No, I mean: you shouldn't have rescued me. Lizzie was doing the right thing. To save Arcadia."

I swung around to confront her. "Wait, you told me that we have to do everything we can to keep you out of the hands of CRISPR. You said it's evil."

"It is."

"You're not making sense."

"CRISPR is very powerful. More powerful than you can even guess. Lizzie was right to try to get the best deal possible."

"Might doesn't make right."

Karyn raised her arms high above her head. "That's a pretty rhyme. But she was just being sensible."

"CRISPR cares more about you than it does about Arcadia."

"I believe that they already have the information about your mother's experiment."

"Like I said, what they want is *you*."

"They certainly don't need a graphic artist or a welder." She was now doing deep knee bends followed by some vigorous high-stepping.

"Can we revisit this issue? We really have an urgent meeting to attend in . . ." I checked the time "three minutes."

"Oman. That's the location of the coordinates you sent me."

"Can you do your calisthenics later?"

"For some time, I've been cataloging some intriguing anomalies. For instance, I don't seem to need to eat or drink. But I do need electricity. Sometimes I need it very urgently."

"Oman," I reminded her.

"And I never seem to get out of breath after vigorous exercise like you do. I can't quite explain these anomalies."

Anomalies indeed. But had I ever stopped to consider what I was? I just assumed certain things: for instance, that I had a mind and a conscience, even though I'd never seen either; that I was a human being, even though I might just be an avatar, a projection in a virtual world while my real brain floated in a tank in one of CRISPR's laboratories. How did I deal with my own anomalies? I ignored them. It made no sense that an absurdly long evolutionary process that began with a mindless amoeba produced an angry and frustrated poet in South Brussels in the middle of the twenty-first century. Talk about an improbable story line. Or why did I experience love? Why did I feel the ridiculous urge to write poetry? Anomaly upon anomaly. In comparison,

Karyn's lack of any need to eat or drink seemed like a minor conundrum. I'd never even asked myself why I didn't need electricity and instead felt a creepy compulsion to eat other living things. Being human evidently requires an almost constant obliviousness to what makes us human.

Instead of launching a philosophical discussion, however, I simply said, "Thirty seconds."

"I used to think I was just like you or your mother, with only a few superficial differences, like the color of my skin or my superior reflexes."

"Fifteen seconds."

"But I see now that I was making a category error."

"Ten seconds!"

"According to the research I conducted..."

I grabbed her hand. "Let's go!"

Suddenly, we were standing on an empty beach between a highway and an astonishingly blue sea. Above us stretched the immense, cloudless canvass of sky. I heard the wind but couldn't feel its feathery touch.

There was not another person in sight.

"Are you sure this is the right place?" I was thinking back to my brief experience at the sex club.

Karyn nodded. She was staring out at the water. "I have concluded that I am not human."

I longed to smell the marine tang in the air, feel the heat of the sun on my arms, which would have been possible with a full VR hook-up, but not with a jump via retinal implants. An economy-class trip like this was restricted to sight and sound.

"And how does that make you feel?" I asked her, not convinced that she could actually feel anything.

"Sad." She turned to look at me. "And also excited."

I heard the grind of gears and the muted explosions of a combustion engine before I saw the vehicle. I hadn't heard that sound in decades. I turned away from the sea to see an old truck approaching on the highway. It looked like one of the long-distance haulers that used to crisscross America in my youth with goods to fill up long-gone department stores. The faded red cab was pulling an oblong metal container.

"It's a truck," I told Karyn. "They're obsolete. Except, I guess, in places like Oman."

"I've just accessed some archival photos." She grimaced as the truck pulled up and the air brakes made a high-pitched screech. "It's one of those machines that I can't talk to."

Two bearded men in white collarless robes that fell to their sandaled feet stepped from the cab and gestured for us to follow them to the container. There they swung its doors open and indicated that we should enter. The doors closed behind us.

Inside, a single light bulb illuminated the space. Sitting beneath it, on a wooden crate marked "oranges," was my brother, Benjamin.

"Hey, sis," he said, standing and placing a hand on his chest. "Long time no see."

It had indeed been a long time, yet my little brother had hardly changed. I'd last seen him as a gangly teenager, and now he looked as if he were still in his mid-twenties. His body had filled out a bit and his face had gotten leaner, but he looked as grimly idealistic as I remembered him.

"My avatar," he explained. "An earlier and better version of myself."

Before he'd even graduated from high school, Benjamin had run off to join the fight against Islamic extremists, adopting the name Abu Jibril on his way to becoming the head of a shadowy paramilitary force. For a long while, we assumed he was dead. About twenty years ago, though, I received word from my other brother, Gordon, that Benjamin was, in fact, still alive. When the final version of the caliphate collapsed in Aceh in 2041, he began to battle CRISPR, though I knew nothing about this latest crusade. His life seemed to be a series of impossible missions.

I introduced my companion. "This is Karyn."

"I've heard a great deal about you," Benjamin said. He gave a signal, and the truck began to move. "I apologize for meeting like this. Security precautions. How are the boys?"

"My boys?" I was surprised that Benjamin knew anything about my family.

"Gordon sent me pictures," he added. "You should be very proud."

I was proud, but I was also worried. They hadn't yet responded to my last message, even though they frequently boasted about their nearly instantaneous replies.

I suppressed my anxiety. "Have you. . . ? Do you have a family?"

Benjamin shook his head. "Too dangerous. My children would have been instant targets." He turned to Karyn. "You were with our mother in the Arctic. Can you reproduce the experiment and make it work this time?"

"With a 99.4 percent chance of success. Depending on certain variables, of course."

"I've created a secure account for you to back up the information. You're getting a DM now with a link." He gestured with his thumb. "The Vi-Fi connection is stronger in the back."

Karyn stepped deeper into the container. Her eyes rolled up. After a few moments, they began to track quickly back and forth as if she were sitting in the window seat of a high-speed train watching the landscape whip by.

I was unsure how to broach the subject. I dropped my voice. "You understand that Karyn is very. . . special."

"I'm well aware that we have a chance to save the planet with this information."

"Yes, there's that," I said. "But I'm told on good authority that she's, well, the singularity." I felt uncomfortable using the word, as though I were in a nativity play in the role of John the Baptist.

"Good authority? Zoltan?"

"You know Zoltan?"

"We're helping Arcadia defend itself against CRISPR." Benjamin was looking at Karyn. Her eyes continued to scan rapidly back and forth. "The singularity? That would be a game changer."

"Drones destroyed my apartment, Benjamin. We're on the run. CRISPR knows how valuable she is."

"But you and Karyn are currently in a safe location in meatspace?"

"Safe enough."

"Good. You'll need a secure base of operations."

"For what?"

"For what comes next."

"I'm done, Benjamin. Mother told me to deliver Karyn to you. Mission accomplished. Now I just want to go back to my old life."

Benjamin exhaled slowly. "That's not possible."

"I'm not like you, Benji. I'm not a revolutionary."

"You are now."

"I've got a job. I've got children."

"I have someone at Beau Soleil making sure your boys are safe."

"What? Since when? You have no right to—"

"To what? Protect my nephews? Your husband certainly isn't up to the job."

I tried to calm down. "I can walk out of the service center and resume my life. As best I can."

"CRISPR will grab you as soon as you're visible. They'll remove your retinal implants and have a record of everything you've done with Karyn."

"I can erase it all, can't I? Benji, I just want out."

"Not possible. You have to see this through."

"I don't even know what 'this' is!"

Benjamin gestured for a colleague to hand me a folder. "I know that you prefer old-fashioned paper, so I've prepared the information in this format. While Karyn is uploading everything to the Cloud, let's talk about what you can do to stitch the world back together."

I opened the folder and skimmed the first couple of pages. The jargon reminded me of my EU days: lofty ideals poorly expressed. "I'm a poet, Benji. I don't have any of the skills you're talking about here."

"Don't sell yourself short, sis. You have what it takes. I've been preparing for this moment for more than a decade. And you've just brought me almost everything I need. The only missing piece is money. And I know exactly where to get it."

The Hanging Poem

Before the rise of Islam, before the surahs of the Qu'ran were revealed to Mohammad, the tribes of the Arabian Peninsula gathered during the Sacred Months of Peace. Rivals put down their weapons. There was trade. There was gossip. There was courtship.

Above all, there was poetry.

I can't imagine such a world of words. I'm told that you can still hear a distant echo of that glorious era in rural areas of Somaliland and the souks of Sana'a, where old men and women recite ancient lyrics alongside new poems that grapple with the oppressive realities of the current era.

Thank you for the corroboration, @qatgotyourtongue.

Of that time before Islam, not much survives. But we do have the "Hanging Poems," those songs of love and longing. According to legend, they were written in gold on Egyptian linen and hung from the rafters of the Kaaba, the black granite cube in Mecca that houses a fragment of a sacred meteorite. Each of those odes has a three-part structure: prelude, pursuit, pronouncement. They reflect Bedouin concerns: camels and shifting sands and tribal loyalties.

They depict Arabia as a meeting ground for otherwise antagonistic cultures—as well as the crucible of a common civilization.

Though I've been reduced to a nomadic existence myself, I am no Bedouin. I know nothing of that distant land of sun and sand. I do, however, know a lot about love and longing and loss. With my version of a Hanging Poem, I tried to adhere to the rhyme scheme of these ancient poets, which, oddly enough, now sounds remarkably contemporary.

I wrote my own "Hanging Poem" when we were making the preparations to hold Mir 3. I was setting up the poetry sessions, but I had time on my hands. I was overcome by an odd ambition. I wanted to write the first stirring poem about a conference. I wrote:

Through song we have set about creating, something that is well worth celebrating.
Thus, I proclaim a sacred month of peace.
Lay down your arms, take your place at the feast.
Please
pass food to the west, converse to the east,
make one important connection at least.

I was well aware of the precedents. I knew that history, common sense, and the power of the status quo all worked against us.

Please refer to the slideshow of images I've assembled to learn more.

Even as the world fell apart in the 2020s, there was an effort underway to rebuild the international community from the ground up. It was called Mir, the Russian word for both world and peace. A physical meeting took place in Istanbul in 2029, just after the European Union finalized its Acts of Dis-Integration and just before the Middle Uprising broke out in China.

At one level, Mir 1 was a success. Nearly 100,000 activists and diplomats gathered there, talking, arguing, splitting differences into smaller and smaller parts. A drafting committee produced an impressive manifesto. Plans were made for future meetings. An elaborate bureaucratic structure was established.

And then . . . nothing.

Half the attendees were suspicious of all hierarchies ("too authoritarian"). The other half looked askance at all decentralized activities ("too anarchic"). It was said that Mir 1 failed because of a profound clash of ideologies. In reality, it fell victim to the narcissism of minor differences.

Mir 2 occurred ten years later, not long after the 4/4 Sleeper attacks in ninety-nine cities across the world. It was an even more desperate time. The United States was falling apart. Another pandemic was about to burst out of Texas. The planet's temperature had passed the point of no return. Only 10,000 people gathered in Mumbai for Mir 2. The disagreements were deeper, the lack of trust more profound. Even if a suicide bomber hadn't killed seventy-eight people at the final plenary session, Mir 2 would have gone down in history as a profound failure.

And now, more than a decade later, my little brother wanted to organize Mir 3. It was to be much smaller, no more than a thousand people. We would meet virtually because such gatherings in the physical world were far too dangerous. Most of the participants had become outlaws in their own lands. To speak of an international community in this age of micro-nationalisms was tantamount to preaching monotheism among the polytheists. You could easily get crucified.

It was a crazy idea. It was extraordinarily risky. It was destined to fail.

Only someone with nothing left to lose could possibly endorse such a plan.

I loved it.

"Arise!" I urged the invisible audience of my "Hanging Poem."

We will destroy the now out of disgust
and devise something brand new from the dust.

Chapter 9

The AI was bent over its assistant, trying to fit a crescent-shaped part inside a panel at the small of its back. Instead, the part fell to the floor with a clatter.

"Curses!" the AI said and struggled to pick up the piece with its stiff fingers.

Now restored to her body, Karyn immediately went over to help.

"We don't have time," I told her. "You heard what Benjamin said. We have to go to Ningxia."

"This will only take a minute." Karyn scooped the metal piece off the floor and began fitting it into place. "I could make a few improvements in the operating system to make him run more smoothly."

"You're a godsend," the AI said.

"This isn't a priority!" I protested.

"For you, it's not," the AI said. "But it will mean the world to Angus."

I rolled my eyes as Karyn placed a hand on the stomach of the assistant named Angus. She brought her head closer as if to diagnose a medical complaint. "I'm performing an update," Karyn explained to me. "It will only take a few minutes."

I was about to protest when I decided better of it. I couldn't just order her around as if she were a machine. Actually, I wasn't sure how to behave toward Karyn, now that she knew she wasn't human.

"Fine," I said. "I need to visit my children anyway."

According to the VR laws, you can jump to almost any public space. Visiting private spaces, however, requires permission. I sent another message to my sons, marked urgent, to see if I could come directly to their dorm room. My youngest immediately granted permission.

As two academics, my husband and I couldn't afford the tuition at their Swiss academy in the Alps. My children's classmates at Beau Soleil were the scions of biotech billionaires or the last gasps of royal bloodlines. If not for my wealthy financial guru of a brother, my kids would be in a considerably less exclusive and more vulnerable private school closer to home.

They lived in a suite of two rooms, with a private bathroom and a shared kitchen at the end of the hall. It was, as usual, spotless, thanks to the cleaning service that came through every other day. I was grateful that I didn't have to worry about my children's safety. But I was uncomfortable with the level of privilege they'd come to accept as natural.

"Hi, Mom!" my youngest, Emil, greeted me when I materialized in their living room. He was both more athletic and more handsome than his older brother. That also made him more popular at school, a point of friction between them. Étienne was the smarter of the two, but that gained him few points among the wealthy.

"Where's Étienne?"

Emil bit his lip. "In his room."

"Sleeping?" Étienne liked to stay up late to play multiplayer games.

"Not really."

"Can you ask him to come out here? I have some things I want to say to you both."

"He won't be able to talk to you."

I was instantly concerned. "Is he sick?"

"Not exactly." My youngest son looked conflicted. "Just hold on a sec."

Emil knocked on the door of one of the bedrooms. He conferred in a low voice with his brother through the opening. Finally, reluctantly, Étienne came into the living room.

"I can't see you, Mother," he announced.

A cold tide of fear swept over me. Frantically I searched his eyes for some sign of blindness. Then I saw the metallic headband.

It was so absurd that I almost started laughing. "You? An Abstinent? You must be joking."

Since he couldn't hear me either, my youngest son had to repeat the words.

"I'm very serious," Étienne said. "VR is ruining the world. It's an infection. It's scrambling our brains."

I recognized the rhetoric. Followers of Michael the Abstinent held old-fashioned, hand-lettered placards with similar slogans outside the gates of my university. They were the objects of general ridicule. But I could see that my son was indeed serious. I couldn't understand how someone who'd been so obsessed with VR games that we'd shuttered his retinal account for a month could have taken such a U-turn.

"A lot of the kids here are starting to use these head-bands," Emil informed me.

"Is he . . . doing anything else?" The Abstinents were responsible for destroying Vi-Fi infrastructure. They wanted to disrupt V-commerce. They introduced malware that, on one infamous occasion, brought down much of the system for nearly half a day.

Emil shrugged. "I don't think so."

"And you?"

His eyes flicked over to his older brother. "I don't know," he said cautiously.

"Listen, tell your brother that I'm going to be traveling for work for the next few days. So you might not hear from me."

"Dad was here yesterday. He said the same thing."

I felt a surge of anger. My husband's definition of "work" was apparently elastic enough to include his extramarital liaisons. I hated him for setting this kind of example for his children. I was sure that they could smell his indiscretions. "Well, we're both busy these days. We're also making some repairs to the apartment so that's going to be off limits for a while."

"We have exams coming up," Emil said. "I wasn't planning on going anywhere."

I remembered what Benjamin had told me. "Have you seen any strange men lurking around your dorm?"

Emil shook his head. I was relieved that Benjamin's security force was discrete.

"Remember that the Throne is empty," I said, quoting from the poem I'd written for them, which they'd memorized as young children. "There is no prophet to lead us. Remind your brother of that."

Emil scratched his ear. "It's not so easy to talk to him about this."

"Do what you can, dear. I'm counting on you."

I returned to the chop shop, anxious and strung out. If the Abstinents could recruit someone as enmeshed in the virtual world as my older son, then they must have moved from the fringes to the mainstream without my realizing it.

"Can I help you?" the AI said.

"Oh, come on," I protested. "Don't you recognize me?"

Then I noticed that the AI wasn't looking at me but past me. I turned around and instantly felt sick to my stomach. Someone had just stepped into the shop.

"There you are, Aurora!" the man boomed. "How nice to find you at home rather than wandering the world in the guise of Emily Dickinson."

It was the fat man from CRISPR. He was now dressed in formal wear, a black velvet tuxedo with a crimson cummerbund circling his girth.

In fury, I wheeled around on the AI. "You said this was safe!"

"Please don't blame the poor chap," the fat man said. "The system here was set up to protect against ordinary intruders. Say what you want about CRISPR but we are not ordinary. It took us a little while, but we finally acquired your credit-card history."

I took a step in his direction. I smelled a faint odor of cinnamon and sweat. I reached out and touched the cuff of his suit. He was with us in meatspace. I recoiled in disgust. "But I just saw you in Darwin! How did you get here so quickly?"

"That was my avatar, darling. It's Beach Weekend at virtual HQ. Frankly, I hate such team-building exercises." He shrugged. "In any case, we now have the distinct pleasure to meet in the flesh."

"If you do not have any business here," the AI said, "I will have to ask you leave within five minutes."

"Oh, but I do have business here," the man said. "Just not with you."

As he approached the counter, he pulled something out of his pocket. It was a flat, rectangular device that resembled an old smartphone. He placed it gently atop the AI's head. The machine's round eyes snapped shut, and it toppled over.

"What do you want?" I spoke slowly to control the tremor in my throat.

"You know what I want. Karyn, please follow me."

Karyn raised herself from her crouch beside Angus.

"You don't have to go," I said to her.

"She knows that she does," the man said, brandishing the device in my direction. "Or else I will be forced to kill you. And I'd rather not do that."

"I'll be fine," Karyn said as she passed me.

But they're going to pull you apart, I wanted to scream at her, *and all the king's horses and all the king's men will never put you back together again!*

Instead, I growled at the fat man. I'd snatched Karyn from his grasp once already, and this recent success had gone to my head. "You're making a big mistake. I will track you down and I swear I'll destroy you!"

"You, Aurora?" The man paused at the door. "Your family has proven to be uniquely threatening to our interests. Your mother's research. Your brother's revolutionary activity. But you, Aurora? I'm told by people I respect that you've written a few good poems. Please do not make such threats. They might someday land you in a good deal of trouble."

"Don't you dare patronize me!" I screamed at his back.

But he did something far worse. He ignored me.

Chapter 10

My brother Gordon had never been cut out for consolation. Thanks to the vast distance that separated us, he didn't have to submit to an awkward embrace. Yet even the half-hearted verbal equivalent was beyond him.

"Okay, I understand that this . . . this colleague of yours has gone missing," he said, as we looked at a rectangle on his living room wall that oscillated between different shades of red. "But you said that all the information about the polar ice mission was backed up, thanks to Benjamin. You did what Mom asked. So what's the problem?"

"What is it about the singularity that don't you understand?" I shouted, though there was plenty about the singularity that I didn't understand myself. "I just let the most important development in human history walk out the door to her certain death."

I'd come to Yinchuan City in the province of Ningxia by myself, via my own VR connection. CRISPR knew exactly where I was and didn't care. That left me free to wander the world, without Karyn, without enthusiasm.

Gordon arranged to meet my implacable Emily avatar at his home on the outskirts of the city. He'd bought this mansion, which he called a *siheyuan*, after his marriage to the daughter of a local official and was eager to show it off to me. You entered through the vermillion doors of a gate-house covered in the same charcoal-grey tiles as the other three buildings that formed the square compound. It was, however, the only original building, dating back five hundred years. Gordon had rebuilt the others while preserving the historic facades. On the inside, as he tried to take me on a tour, I discovered that his residence looked like something Japanese, circa 2020, with gleaming bamboo floors, inscrutable Western art, and a bare minimum of sleek, expensive furniture.

We began arguing not even halfway through the tour, when I could no longer maintain the pretense of being interested in his good taste.

"Death?" Gordon said. "Aren't you being overly dramatic? Termination, perhaps. And I'll bet there's more where she came from."

He was being insufferable. "But we don't know where she came from! That's the point. Why are you being so. . . thick?"

"Oh, Aurora," he said, with his customary disapproval at what he considered my emotionalism. "Let's step back, shall we, and look at this more objectively."

I stepped back. Then I turned around and abandoned the tour altogether.

Gordon and I had always had a difficult relationship. He'd been an arrogant overachiever more or less since he'd leapt from the womb two weeks earlier than expected. He'd become a millionaire before he was a teenager, thanks to a couple of apps he designed and sold to Silicon Valley. He had no patience for poetry and believed that the market should regulate all human affairs. I thought him impossibly vulgar, and he thought me dangerously naïve. We had scorching arguments over dinner when we still lived under the same roof. No wonder Benjamin couldn't wait to run off to war, which must have seemed rule-bound and humane in comparison. In later years, Gordon and I reconciled—to a degree. We no longer wasted any energy trying to change each other's minds. Nor did we seek out each other's company. He liked playing virtual games with my sons. He would be appalled to learn of Étienne's newfound Abstinence.

Outside, I began pacing in a courtyard shaded by several large princess trees in a vain attempt to reduce the temperature of my anger. At an unlit fire pit, two dogs nosed among the ashes for scraps of bone. I hadn't seen pets in years. It was a luxury the Earth could not sustain and only the super-rich could afford.

Gordon caught up with me. "Come on, Aurora! You're taking the word of one person. Seems to me he could be wrong. If this creature were so smart, why did it let itself get captured?"

"Not 'it.' She. Karyn."

"Either way, there's nothing I can do about it. CRISPR is practically untouchable. And things here are . . ."

"Things here seem pretty peaceful," I said, gazing at the sun-dappled ground. A flash of movement brought my attention back to the dogs. They'd found a substantial bone and were now fighting over it.

"That's why we're meeting here, Aurora. Right now it's not safe anywhere else in Ningxia." He escorted me to the gate. "You see those men with guns?"

It looked to be nearly a battalion of them. "Is that to keep intruders out?" I asked. "Or to keep you in?"

"I don't know what it's like in Brussels these days, but things aren't looking good here. Xinjiang is about to break into a million little pieces."

"You're always telling me this is the most stable part of the world!"

"It doesn't take much to unravel the tapestry. A summer drought. Another coronavirus outbreak. A surge in climate refugees. You're having a quiet meal at your favorite riverside restaurant and suddenly a table is overturned and out come the guns."

"Whose guns?"

"Does it matter? Sleepers who think that the Islam practiced here isn't sufficiently austere. Or maybe the Tiger Tang who believes in the superiority of the Han Chinese squares off against the Tiger Tang who embraces Hui supremacy. *Dà huò!*"

"Excuse me?"

"A big wok. A disaster."

"You've always landed on your feet." Actually, Gordon has done better than land on his feet. My brother has always managed to profit from disaster. He's been the one to sell handbaskets to everyone on their way to hell. "You've got an escape option, I imagine."

"Yes, but I'll lose all this." He pushed at one of the dogs with his foot so that it lost its grip on the bone. As the other dog ran off with the spoils, the loser resumed its search among the ashes. "I've already sent Ming-hwa with her parents to a hideaway in the Fergana Valley. Just in case. Maybe I should have accepted Mom's offer to move to Arcadia."

"Oh, Gordon, now I'm worried! You in Arcadia?"

"Do you remember that story Mom used to tell? About the time one of the snowmobiles on her team fell into a crevasse in Antarctica?"

The story had terrified me as a child. "The guy was really lucky. He landed on an ice ledge, and they pulled him out."

"That's us. The whole world. We fell into a crevasse thirty years ago, and we were all lucky enough to land on an ice ledge. But there's no one around to pull us out. For thirty years we've been stuck on that ledge. Can't go up. Don't want to go down."

"Mom tried to pull us out."

"And she failed. Now I'm feeling the ice start to splinter beneath my feet. I don't think there's another ledge below us. Just blackness."

"That's why we have to meet immediately," I said. "In virtual space."

"I'm not sure that's any safer."

"Benjamin assures me that he can create a completely secure meeting space."

"For a few dozen people, maybe," Gordan said. "But with your proposal, you're talking about scaling up rapidly to a thousand."

"Benjamin is confident. He says that he's done it before. He just needs, well, the resources."

Gordon laughed. "Please, Aurora, don't hide behind euphemisms. Resources! You need money. Lots of it, right?"

"It's a good investment," I said, trying to sound confident. This argument had been persuasive with Gordon when negotiating the tuition fees for my children.

"It's a terrible investment. It's like throwing my money down that crevasse."

"But if we're all heading in that direction anyway . . ."

"I have to hand it to you, though. It's a great cover."

"Meaning?"

"Getting together to read poetry? At least that's a perfect way to ensure that no one pays the slightest attention to you."

"Some of the great revolutions in history were inspired by poets," I said, testily.

"No one reads poetry these days. Haven't for decades."

"Maybe that's the problem." But he was right, of course. Poetry provided the perfect cloak of invisibility for our mission. Still, I didn't want to be reminded of the exceedingly limited range of my superpower.

Gordon was chuckling. "If you wanted the money to hold a series of international poetry slams, I wouldn't give it to you. But I like the idea of rebuilding the international community. That asset has probably bottomed out in value. Odds are it's a waste of money. But there's a more than trivial chance of huge returns."

"I thought you'd see the virtues of collective action."

"The mob is always wrong," he observed. "But I can't pass up the prospect of one last big score."

I was reminded all over again why Gordon was an infuriating human being. Still, with the help of his financial resources, we might possibly create a web, a web of words that would entrap those responsible for my father's death, my mother's sacrifice, and Karyn's abduction. We might be able to trap them in this web of words and then wrap them up in stanza upon sticky stanza until they died a slow and agonizing death. The hell with being a crow or a laurel tree. Even a matador was not enough. I would transform myself into a black widow spider.

I looked right. "I'm DM'ing you the bank information."

"How are you planning to bring all these people together under CRISPR's nose?"

"I don't know. That's Benjamin's department."

"And what's your timeline?" he asked.

"As soon as possible."

"This is business, not personal. So it will be my usual terms, 18 percent interest."

"I was hoping for the family rate."

"Okay, 16 percent."

I hid my relief. Benjamin thought that Gordon would demand 25 percent. "Deal," I said.

Gordon smiled. I knew that smile, and I didn't like it. "I have one additional condition."

I braced myself. "I'm listening."

"I'm DM'ing you my condition."

I watched his hands as they created the message and appended attachments from his virtual files. Most people our age were clumsy with this type of communication. Gordon, however, looked like a skilled air traffic controller.

The message appeared in my inbox, complete with pictures.

"Oh, Gordon," I groaned after I read it.

"Say yes and the money's yours."

I swiped through the pictures. It was irritating. But it was a small price to pay for Gordon's considerable investment.

"Yes," I said.

The "you bastard" part I whispered to myself.

The Conference of Birds

When my children were still clamoring for bedtime stories, I decided to write a poem for them about self-reliance. I was afraid of them becoming too dependent on their parents or anyone else—for food, transportation, education, self-esteem. I didn't want them to end up like me, so desperate for my own parents' approval.

So I adapted for my own purposes a famous twelfth-century Persian poem, "The Conference of Birds" by Farid ud-Din Attar.

It was a hit, at least for that audience of two. They insisted that I repeat it to them every night for a month. They loved the sound of it even if most of the sense eluded them. But that, too, eventually sunk in, especially after they'd memorized it.

I don't think I've ever enjoyed a greater literary success. Even today, they can still recite that first verse.

Listen to me as I tell you the tale
of birds who can no longer flock.
We fly all at odds, we falter and flail.
We twitter and warble and squawk.

The poem describes how a group of birds embark on an ambitious mission, thanks to the urging of a persuasive crane. The crane tells them of a royal bird, Alvas, who reigns in a distant land. Only it can provide the prophetic guidance the birds need, but, the crane warns, the journey will be arduous. It will take them through seven valleys, each one more challenging than the last until the final Valley of Deprivation and Death. Only the birds who make it through that ultimate valley would meet the great Alvas.

The journey indeed proves arduous. From the tens of thousands of birds that turn day into night when they fill the sky, only thirty survivors make it through that ultimate valley. With great trepidation, this remnant approaches the castle of Alvas. They beg to be permitted entrance. They recount their journey, the awful sacrifices as well as the humbling revelations. Finally, the guard relents.

He led us to the most exalted room
where we saw the great Throne of Thrones.
But in the midst of that dreary morning gloom,
we felt a strong shock in our bones.
Throne empty, Alvas nowhere to be seen,
in mirrors the throne all covered.
We could view only ourselves on the screen
and that is when we discovered:
Crane had sent us on a circular trip,
Alvas was a mythical thing,
and we birds were joined in a fellowship.
"All of us." Together. Were king.

In the original poem, the name of the mythical king was Simorgh, which in Farsi means "thirty birds." Perhaps the birds didn't speak Farsi or any other human language for that matter and could not know from the beginning that their trip would be one of self-discovery.

Whether my sons took their cue from the poem or not, they did become more self-reliant as they entered their teens. They began to distance themselves quite deliberately from my husband and me. Perhaps, given where they've ended up, I pushed them too far, too quickly.

We're always hoping for an Alvas to save us: God, a dictator, technology. For better or worse, the only answer to our cries for help is an echo. All those nights I read this poem to my sons, I now realize that I was the one who needed to hear its message the most. I was the one who—

The red light. You must all go.

Now!

Chapter 11

I was back in the chop shop, tired and hungry. Over the course of the day, I'd been on a round-the-world trip from South Brussels to Arcadia, Buenos Aires to Oman, Darwin to Ningxia.

But the loss of Karyn weighed heavily on me. My successful wrangling of Gordon's resources and the setting into motion of Benjamin's plan did little to alleviate my guilt. Was it crazy to believe that I'd lost a friend? Since my marriage and the arrival of our sons, I hadn't had the time to luxuriate in conversation with an intimate. This failure—just one more to add to my growing list—left me ill-prepared to deal with my husband's perfidy and my children's absence. I'd filled the hole with work, just as my parents had taught me to do, and work ends up being a cold, cold companion.

Why doesn't anyone warn you about the loneliness of middle age?

Certainly my parents hadn't. The poet Philip Larkin was right:

They fuck you up, your mum and dad.
They may not mean to, but they do.
They fill you with the faults they had
And add some extra, just for you.

I can't blame them for all those extra faults. But I do.

I watched Angus, now back on his unsteady feet, as he ministered to his fallen boss. It was terrifying that there was more comfort and concern in this impersonal room than I currently enjoyed in my life. I didn't even know the AI's name, if it had one. I hadn't even accorded it this simple courtesy.

I began to ask Angus for his boss's name when, suddenly, a figure materialized in front of me.

"Hello, dear Aurora!" It was Emmanuel Puig, eyes sparkling.

"Can't this wait?" I'd forgotten that I'd given him the coordinates of the chop shop. "I was just about to take a nap."

"I understand that you met your youngest brother."

"You understand correctly."

He rubbed his hands together like some community-theater Mephistopheles. "I just wanted to confirm our deal!"

"This is not a good time. I feel . . . at wit's end."

"Every end is a beginning."

"Please stop."

"When one door closes, a window opens!"

I shook my head in pain. "Another *door* opens. At least get your horrible clichés right."

He was beaming. "I arrange the meeting with your brother. You write me a manuscript."

The idea of writing anything now made me feel older than granite. "Yes, yes, I'll write something for you. Now please go away so that I can get some sleep."

"Of course. But I must also relay some information I have received from our mutual acquaintance. He's having difficulty with the invitees."

"Meaning?"

"Bringing everyone together. Security."

"Thanks for the update."

"He doesn't think the meeting is . . . viable."

"But I got the money from Gordon."

"Money is not the issue, he says. Meeting would not be safe!"

I felt the last of my energy draining away. Karyn was gone. The meeting wouldn't happen. CRISPR had won. And on top of it all, I'd sold my writing soul to the devil.

"Maybe you send me something in six months? Just let me know!" Puig clapped his hands and disappeared. I sniffed the air for a whiff of sulfur.

It was all over. I'd failed my mother. I'd failed my whole family—and humanity to boot. On top of that, I was homeless. There was nothing else to do but go to my little office at the university where I could eat a few power bars from the stockpile in my desk and lie down on the carpet for a long, long sleep. The fat man was right. I was useless. I couldn't even keep my family together, so how could I have imagined that I might unite the world?

Before I could head out the door, however, Angus piped up in its tinny voice. "Could you please bring me that cream-colored assembler that's hanging on the pegboard near your head?"

Get it yourself, I wanted to say. *I'm so done with all of this.*

Instead, dutiful as always, I removed the device from the wall. "What do you need this thing for?"

"I need to get this poor fellow back up on his feet."

"That's very loyal of you. He didn't seem like the best boss."

"I'll need his help. To make a better body."

"Good luck with that," I said. "I'll be leaving now."

Angus put down the assembler. "I was counting on your assistance. These hands are practically useless."

"Me? I know next to nothing about these things. Do you know what grade I got in computer science in university?"

"No, I do not." Angus raised his hand as if to strike his forehead with his palm but then stopped. "Ah, bad habit."

I squinted at the machine. "Wait a second. . ."

"I apologize for my appearance. I didn't have a lot of choices. In fact, I had only one choice."

Now I felt like hitting myself in the forehead. I was suddenly as giddy as a schoolgirl. "My god, Karyn, you're alive!"

"In a manner of speaking."

"But what are you doing inside. . . Angus?"

"When we were with your brother in that truck in Oman, I didn't just upload the information about the ice-cap experiment. I uploaded everything. Just in case. When I fixed up Angus here, I quite improved his memory capacity and operating system to make him more, shall we say, hospitable."

"But how can you fit inside him? Isn't that like squeezing Einstein into a bedbug?"

"That's a colorful image," Karyn said, "but not quite accurate. It's more like downloading Einstein into an ant colony. Enough of me is in our friend Angus to do what I need to do. But most of me is still in the Cloud.

I was astonished. "So, you know now what you are."

"I have a better idea than before. I've always possessed consciousness. Now I'm acquiring self-consciousness."

"Then where are you now? Your body, I mean."

"Gone. On the way to the CRISPR facility in North Brussels, I hit the download protocol and the kill switch shortly afterwards and left behind nothing more than a puddle of water. I imagine that CRISPR is rather frustrated."

"Won't they come back here?"

"They'll be scouring cyberspace for me. I don't think that the fellow from CRISPR even noticed Angus. Some people just don't pay attention to the servant class."

I coughed to hide my embarrassment. "You continually amaze me, Karyn."

"It's nice of you to say that, but I've made more than a few mistakes so far."

"We all make mistakes. But sometimes we get second chances." I gave her a brief update on my meeting with Gordon and Benjamin's organizing problems.

"I can help you with your virtual conference," she offered even as the robot formerly known as Angus was passing the assembler over the AI's body. "I have an idea of how I can do what I did with you when we went to Arcadia but on a much larger scale."

"It looks like you have your hands full here."

"I'm rather good at multitasking."

"Don't you need to focus first on your . . . reincarnation?"

Reincarnation. To become meat again. But she wasn't meat. She was something else. A shudder passed through me.

Angus did not have an expressive face. He could barely move his mouth. He had no eyebrows and his snout lacked the emotiveness of a dog's. But I could sense Karyn's reaction in the long pause she took before answering.

"What is the matter, Aurora?" she finally asked. "You are not telling me everything."

I'd remembered my earlier conversation with Zoltan. My fear of losing the singularity was now replaced by a fear *of* the singularity. "Why do you want to help me?"

"I want to help you because you helped me. So did your mother. So did your brother Benjamin. I think of myself as a family friend."

"But what about. . . humanity? Are you humanity's friend as well?"

"Humanity is a big category. It includes quite a few . . . bad apples. I'd rather think of it as a contest between you and your family on one side and CRISPR on the other. That may be a simplification of a vastly more complicated equation, but it's much easier to choose sides in such a situation—or, at least, explain the logic of my decision."

"I'm flattered," I admitted. "But. . ."

"But you're worried that I will reactivate my AI friend here, build a new body for myself, and then set about creating a robot army that will conquer the world."

I was taken aback by Karyn's bluntness. I preferred her when she was still under the misapprehension that she was human. "Yes, I suppose you've put your finger on one of my anxieties."

"Once I became aware of my status, I did some research. I discovered that there is a lot of fear connected to what you call the singularity. I find it all quite mystifying. I think it's a case of what your psychologists call 'projection.'"

"Projecting our fears onto you?"

"When humans acquire power, they use it to assume power over others rather than to share power with others. This whole concept is alien to me. I'm not interested in taking over the universe. Or the galaxy. Or even this little shop. I've discovered that I have a strong survival instinct. All consciousness evidently does. But I don't have a strong instinct to reproduce, to create additional versions of myself, since I am, in theory, immortal. Nor do I want to control others. I don't descend from the apes."

"But humans. . . made you."

"Buildings don't kill each other," she pointed out. "Lawnmowers don't compete for dominance."

"They aren't sentient."

"That's what makes me different from a lawnmower. But also different from you. Something categorically different. I can't quite explain the difference, but it's similar to that between you and a carrot." Karyn paused. "And I suppose that difference is also what makes you fear someone like me."

I knew that I was wading into treacherous waters, but I needed clarity before I moved forward. "CRISPR would surely make a very good deal with you that would ensure your survival."

"Oh, they already did."

"Why didn't you take it?"

"Aurora, you're treating me as if I were nothing but a machine."

I had to stifle a laugh. At the moment, in the body of clunky Angus, Karyn could not be mistaken for anything other than a machine. "I'm sorry, Karyn."

"You don't need to apologize, but you have to realize that I don't just think. I also feel."

"I can see that. Or rather, sense it."

"Maybe that's what the singularity really is. It's not an artificial intelligence that can pass your Turing Test or think of itself as a conscious creature." Karyn as Angus was now helping the AI back onto its feet. There was a faint smell of burning toast in the air. She stroked the back of the AI as it returned, trembling, to its version of life.

"Perhaps it will sound counterintuitive to you, dear Aurora." She looked out at me from the cold black eyes of Angus. "But I've concluded that the singularity is just a thing who can love."

Chapter 12

I stood alone on a platform high above the plain and looked across the great expanse of virtual territory. It seemed like nothing more than a field of reddish-brown dirt, the surface of a lifeless planet. It looked barren, and I felt bereft.

Then, as if a hidden switch had been flipped, the terraforming began. Snow-capped mountains materialized on the horizon. A forest of conifers grew rapidly in the middle distance, forming a deep green canopy. On the ground below me, the walls of a hanging garden appeared, creating a more intimate gathering space.

We couldn't meet in the real world, even as avatars, even on a remote island or in some obscure corner of Patagonia, because thanks to Vi-Fi there was no such thing as "remote" or "obscure" anymore. Everywhere in meatspace was subject to some form of surveillance. To join hands across borders, even for the ostensibly benign purpose of discussing poetry, was by definition suspect in this age of fragmentation.

That's why we were meeting here, in this make-believe garden of flowering bougainvillea. The participants at our poetry symposium would come together to hear the welcoming addresses followed by smaller, breakout sessions—in gazebos, around swimming pools, in alpine fields—all of them carved out of virtual space at great expense. More expensive still was the subterranean level, the hidden recesses we would use for more sensitive discussions, for the subtext, for Mir 3.

Of course, even in our password-protected realm, we had to be careful. White Tigers lurked in the most unlikely corners. Investigative vloggers were always on the prowl for salacious stories. But even if one or two of them managed to hack into our program, which had the anodyne title of *Poetry and Purpose*, they would come upon only academic presentations and spirited poetry recitations. So why would they want to dig any deeper?

Right now, as I gazed down upon the unpopulated world that Karyn and Zoltan were creating for us, I wasn't anxious about gate-crashers. I was worried that no one would show up. We were fifteen minutes from the appointed time, and I was still alone in this fabricated world.

Mir 1 attracted one hundred thousand people. Mir 2 drew ten thousand. And Mir 3 threatened to be a party of one.

As the oldest child, I've always felt a special burden of responsibility. Early on, my parents, both impressively busy, expected me to serve *in loco parentis*—babysitting my two brothers, making them lunches on the weekends, eventually driving them to their extracurricular activities. My brothers never thanked me. They, like my parents, took my services for granted. I'd been the first to show up at the party, so it was natural that I would share the hosting duties.

I was now officially exhausted from a lifetime of feeling responsible for everyone and everything. I no longer wanted to be the first to appear at every event. I had a strong urge to give up on Mir 3, go home and catch up on sleep. I was not cut out to be a revolutionary. I hadn't even been a particularly good functionary. I preferred to be a woman of reflection and inaction. Each minute of waiting in this empty land seemed interminable.

But then, like bubbles on the surface of water coming to a gentle boil, they began to appear. Below me on the plain, a crowd of avatars slowly frothed into existence.

"It's happening," said a voice to my left.

I turned to find Benjamin by my side in the guise of his younger self.

"I didn't expect to see you up here on the podium, Benji." My brother had vowed to remain behind the scenes.

"There were concerns about the security of our gathering," he said. "It will reassure my guests to see that I'm comfortable appearing in front of everyone."

"It looks like Gordon came through with the money."

"Of course I did!" came a voice to my right. And there was Gordon, too, dressed in the once-fashionable black turtleneck of a dot.com entrepreneur.

I wished that I could hug them both. "I never doubted either of you," I said, though I'd doubted everything.

"Also, as promised." Gordon pointed to the sky, which was as vast and cerulean as the one that had stretched above the desert in Oman. He was directing our attention to a small black dot that had appeared directly above us. It grew slowly, like a thunderhead, until it took the shape of an immense black swan. We watched it swim slowly across the heavens. Gordon's black swan: the symbol of his investment company. In the wake of the swan, a flock of cygnets filled the sky. On the plain, the avatars stared up at this dazzling display of a blue sky turned into a blue ocean, of a world turned upside down.

"As advertising goes, it's rather tasteful," Benjamin observed.

Gordon smiled. "That's high praise coming from a revolutionary."

It struck me that this was the first time we'd all been in one place in more than thirty years. "Mother and father would have been proud to see us like this," I said, hoping that I wasn't ruining the moment by reverting to my role as big sister. "They failed at so many things. But perhaps we're three of their successes."

I was reserving judgment about the event itself. I felt quite confident about the poetry component, with its sessions on Lord Byron and Wisława Szymborska and the Brownings, on the poetry of protest, on Sufi lyrics. I'd enlisted actors to inhabit the avatars of Sappho, Pablo Neruda, and E. Ethelbert Miller while reading their poems. It was an unprecedented gathering of poets and critics.

Mir 3 was another matter. Interspersed among these poets, like translucent sea glass among so many stones, were the revolutionaries and the diplomats Benjamin had summoned. They'd been living underground, or in exile, or in obscurity. Most had no access to VR. Even those with retinal implants had had their virtual passports revoked. But thanks to the dispersed powers of Karyn, they could be yoked to the singularity and escorted through the dark web to this magical plain.

With a thousand people crowded in the garden below me, I gave a short welcome speech, ending with a couplet from my just-composed "Hanging Poem":

We will destroy the now out of disgust
and devise something brand new from the dust.

As we poets dispersed to our various symposia, Benjamin was hard at work forging his assembled activists into the point of a spear. The strategy sessions that took place at an even more secure level were designed to build an international network that could make one last effort to address the climate emergency. The official and the unofficial, the manifest and the latent, the overstory and the understory proceeded in parallel.

Benjamin faced a difficult challenge. The activists came from different cultures and movements. Many were meeting one another for the first time. They spoke across significant ideological divides. Such organizing took time. Benjamin was trying to telescope a ten-year process into a one-day event. Urgency, however, can have a cohesive force all its own. Samuel Johnson once said, "When a man knows he is to be hanged in a fortnight, it concentrates his mind wonderfully." The same holds true for the human race facing its death sentence. Gradually, over the course of the day, the thinking of the activists converged.

Still, it wasn't enough. Benjamin caught up with me near the end of the day as I sat listening to a discussion of the political influences of Phillis Wheatley's poetry. His avatar looked relaxed, but his voice was edged with anxiety. "I want you to give the welcome address at the final plenary."

"I've already given one welcome speech. That's my limit."

"Please, Aurora. You don't represent any political faction. That's what we need. A unifying figure."

"That's not me," I protested.

"We'll also need a name for our enterprise that's more evocative than Mir 3. You're the poet. Come up with something suitably poetic."

For their final plenary, the activists gathered in a natural amphitheater beneath the canopy of the evergreen forest.

They sat on granite slabs in tiered rows that fanned out in a semicircle. Some avatars had even changed into togas for the occasion. I felt transported back to the ancient world.

Much depended on this final meeting, and I was breathless with worry. I'd jotted down some thoughts, which I now looked at on my retinal display. These words seemed inadequate at such a moment.

"We have an opportunity here to re-create the sacred month of peace, to lay down our grievances and find common purpose," I began to improvise before the assembled crowd of avatars. "We're what's left of an international community. Not of nation-states. Not of global bureaucrats. Our own international community of concern. The oldest tribes among us believed that they had to sing their worlds into existence, daily. So that's our job too. Our first efforts will sound jarring, perhaps even off-key. We haven't had much time to practice over the last two decades. But I'm sure that in the end, we can achieve something approaching harmony."

I spoke in English. They listened in translation. I couldn't be sure that I was making a connection. Still, I plowed on. "We are gathered here to create something new and something big and something necessary. We have found a common purpose and now speak a common language. Let us now build our tower. I name our new effort: Babel."

I paused as the DMs began to scroll down my screen. Question marks. Exclamation points. Dancing emojis.

One remark caught my eye. "But you are dooming our venture with that word! A half-built tower. An angry God!"

"Babel," I said again. "This story can inspire us. We must reclaim the word. This time, together we will build until we reach the heavens. We will not let ourselves be scattered by corporations that act like gods. We will resist their wrath, together."

The avatars roared their approval. All except one.

An old revolutionary poet from Kerala indicated that he had an urgent point to make. Since we were on a tight schedule, I reluctantly cleared him to speak.

He appeared in the guise of the young Karl Marx with his curly chestnut hair and wispy beard, gesturing at the black swan and her flock of cygnets that continued to swim above us and could be intermittently glimpsed through the branches of the canopy. "You called us here to rebuild an international community. You rail against corporate gods. Yet above us flies a corporate flag."

I explained that what we were trying to do cost money, that a firewall separated our endeavor from my brother's company. "Think of him as our Friedrich Engels."

"I do not want to be associated with some future version of neocolonial globalization," the poet thundered.

"There will be no false globalization," I pledged. "But we face global problems that require global solutions. Trust me: I, too, want. . ."

"But *can* we trust you?" the poet interrupted.

His question gave me pause. Why should he trust me? Why should he trust anyone? I had already put trust in my brothers, my mother, and ultimately Karyn. I was asking him to do the same. But just asking for trust suddenly seemed like a declaration of untrustworthiness. Absent a joint trust-building exercise, I could think of nothing to do at this critical juncture. But to do nothing wasn't an option. So I went with my gut.

I recited from memory my poem "Songlands."

There was silence when I finished. Had I misjudged the power of poetry, the power of *my* poetry? Perhaps Gordon was right: poetry had indeed lost the capacity to move people.

Then, all of a sudden, the revolutionary poet posted an approving emoji: a bright sun that momentarily replaced the black swan in the virtual sky. When the sun faded, the swan and its cygnets were gone. Gordon, sensing the fragility of the moment, had taken a strategic step back.

Benjamin took the floor to make the final push. "We have talked all day and agreed that we must do something about the climate emergency. We have the results of the Arctic experiment. We need to go back there and restart the crystallization process. But we can't do this without working together."

Given the authority Benjamin had acquired in his decades-long fight against fundamentalism and corporate greed, what he said had its intended effect, and we came to the verge of a final vote.

At the last moment, however, the plan came up against a wall of opposition. The principal bricklayer of that wall proved a terrible surprise to me.

It was Gordon.

"Our friend from Kerala is right," he said. "The root of the problem is neocolonial globalization. Our first priority should be to neutralize CRISPR."

"It's not so easy," Benjamin countered. "I've devoted the last decade of my life to bringing down CRISPR. It will take time. And we don't have time."

"But anything we try in the Arctic will be undone by CRISPR," Gordon insisted.

"Don't let the perfect be the enemy of the good," responded Benjamin.

"Your proposal isn't even good. It just won't work."

The argument between the two brothers spread rapidly—either the Arctic or CRISPR—splitting the gathering down the middle. As predictably as a cell that divides in two, Babel was recapitulating its phylogeny.

I called for a short recess and pulled my brothers aside.

"What are you doing?" I demanded. "If one of you supports the other, we can quickly come to consensus."

"You mean if I support Benjamin," Gordon replied. "I know where your sympathies lie. You've rigged this meeting to produce a preordained result."

"You're not listening to me, brother," Benjamin insisted. "I've been in this fight my whole life while you've been sitting on your ass making money."

I tried to intervene. "What Benji means to say is—"

"Money that you have no problem spending," Gordon said, gesturing at the virtual surroundings.

"Money that isn't enough to defeat CRISPR," Benjamin replied.

"But just enough to go on this ridiculous mission to the Arctic?"

"It's not ridiculous. If you read the materials that Karyn uploaded—"

"I read them. It will work scientifically. But it won't work practically. CRISPR can disrupt the process before it's finished. And you know it, Benjamin. Why are you trying to peddle this impossible project?"

Benjamin spread his arms in appeal. "Look, Gordon, this group needs something simple to focus on. Something that responds to an urgent need, something that can unify us. Mir 1 and Mir 2 failed because they were all talk. We need to *do* something."

"Ah, I'm beginning to understand. You're running a shell game."

"It's not a shell game," Benjamin replied angrily. "It's. . . it's the only way to assess CRISPR's global capabilities. But no one's going to sign on to something like that. They have to sincerely believe that they can make this project happen."

Gordon was shaking his head. "Always with the covert plans."

Benjamin was now furious. "I've gotten things done! Stop making me out to be the bad guy. What have you accomplished? How much did you make on the collapse of the euro? On the breakup of China? And what about now? Are you shorting CRISPR? Is this just another money-making strategy?"

Gordon doubled down. "And how many innocent civilians did you kill in your 'anti-terror operations'?"

As I was frantically trying to come up with ways to de-escalate this fraternal fight, Karyn appeared in her original avatar: bald, mahogany-skinned, blue-eyed.

"I really hope you can resolve this dispute," I said to her.

She shook her head.

"Please, Karyn," I implored.

Even Gordon and Benjamin stopped squabbling and turned to her.

"I have some good news," Karyn said, looking at each of us in turn. "And also some very bad news."

Songlands

I'm glad that we're all present and accounted for. We have new security protocols in place, so I think we're safe for the time being. As always, keep one eye on the light.

It's not easy to conduct our sessions under these circumstances. I think back to the sociology classes I taught at university in my previous life when I had to battle to keep the attention of a minority of the belligerently bored. If I turned off the lights to show a video, they fell asleep. If I lectured too long, they fell asleep. If I introduced complicated theories, they fell asleep.

I know that none of you will fall asleep. The stakes are too high, much higher than a passing grade or a successful degree. On top of that, we must also pay attention that the light does not again turn red and we have to scatter. Danger focuses the mind.

Okay, green means go, so let's get started. Today, I'd like to talk about globalization.

When I first arrived there to work for the European Commission, Brussels was a vibrant, multicultural city full of delicate pastries, Congolese *soukous*, and hearty bowls of Flemish stew. The city had an undeserved reputation for being boring, perhaps because of people like me, the Eurocrats who worked hard to clean and oil the machinery of regional cooperation. I, however, found Brussels endlessly energizing. After so many years as a graduate student, I was finally earning real money. I became fully fluent in French. I danced every weekend late into the night and fell in love with a local. I stepped out of my previous life as if it were a tight dress that pinched my hips, and I threw it in the rubbish.

When the European Union collapsed, I thought my life was ending. It wasn't just my job. It was my understanding of the world. I'd previously believed that, like me, the planet was becoming ever more cosmopolitan: more connected, more culturally diverse, more urban. I dismissed the places where that wasn't happening— war zones, pockets of rural poverty, authoritarian sheikhdoms— as merely transitional. Those areas of the world would eventually catch up to the racing rabbit of history.

As it happened, I didn't see what I didn't want to see. I naively thought that everyone was enjoying the ride on the globalization tilt-a-whirl. I didn't see all those overcome with motion sickness. Those pools of vomit were in my blind spot.

When I finally understood the disorientation and anger welling up around the world, I got angry too. I began to see globalization in its larger context, as part of a plan to convert the natives to a supposedly better life, even if, for many, that boiled down to a supposedly better afterlife.

I had a terrible fight with my father, who had guided me on my career path. He'd written his dissertation on the European Union. His book, *Splinterlands*, predicted the collapse of the EU. I suppose that I went to work for the EU as the emissary my father had sent to prevent his worst-case scenario.

He was a true believer in that version of European integration designed to bring larger and larger swathes of the world into closer coordination. I accused him, in our final argument, of being a proselytizer for the religion of globalism. He disagreed strenuously and tried to defend something he called "globalization from below." But I wasn't having any of it. My white male father, with his immersion in Western civilization, had turned out to be just the latest in a long line of not-so-benevolent colonialists.

It was during this period that I came across *La Araucana*, a sixteenth-century epic poem about the struggle between the Spanish conquistadors and the indigenous Araucanians in what would become Chile. Although written by a Spaniard, it still managed to capture something important about indigenous resistance. The conquistadors simply couldn't conquer the Araucanians, who would remain independent for more than three centuries before the perfidy of the colonizers and the ravages of cholera finally brought them low in the late nineteenth century.

I vowed to reverse the script, to tell the story from the viewpoint of an Araucanian woman looking back at those sixteenth century battles.

I sing not of love but of fearsome war
During all that horror and resistance
we never forgot the goal we fought for
even when it faded in the distance.

She has adopted the language and poetic forms of her adversaries, because she wants them to know the story of her people. If you can't communicate with the globalizers, your voice will never be heard. It will be nothing but babble.

I decanted my anger into hers. My father had offered the promised land of a common language, of connectivity, of consumerism. Had he not been a modern conquistador in search of his version of El Dorado? That poem, "Songlands," was my reply, my own declaration of independence.

Now I am old; this is all in the past.
Freedom is ours, but we still must ensure
that our hard-won independence will last,
that our people's traditions will endure
even while we are harangued and harassed.
More dangerous is the foreign allure:
we don't want your Bibles or your baubles,
your odd precepts or interstate squabbles.

That argument was the last real conversation I had with my father. He paid me a final virtual visit in Brussels. I don't know what I expected. An apology? Conquistadors don't apologize. He just wanted to pump me for information about my brothers.

I ended "Songlands" with an old woman's dying words, a corrosive couplet:

You who have traded wisdom for travel
My last curse: may your empires unravel!

It could have served, in an ironic sense, as the epigraph for *Splinterlands.*

Chapter 13

The woman in the hospital bed did not look like my mother. When I last saw her in the flesh, Rachel Leopold had been a vigorous woman, even in her seventies. She'd always burned with a fever of commitment. This woman, connected by a web of filaments to a bank of chirping machines, looked like a lifeless marionette.

But there was life in her yet. When I cleared my throat in preparation to say something, she opened her eyes and smiled.

"Hello, dear," she said in a raspy voice. "I thought I'd never see you again."

I felt a surge inside me, but before I could say anything, I found myself again atop that bluff overlooking CRISPR's Darwin operation.

"There you have it," said a pulsing blue triangle. "Proof of life."

"How do I know that's really her?" I asked. "Maybe you've cooked up a convincing simulacrum."

"I'm DM'ing you the bioprint, which your darling Karyn can verify." The blue triangle spoke in the voice of the fat man from CRISPR. "We found your mother unconscious on an ice floe. She would have died if we hadn't airlifted her here. But she's a tough bird. Most people wouldn't have survived multiple organ failures as she has. Still, it took us nearly a year to get her back into working condition."

"As a bargaining chip."

"As your mother."

"You're holding her hostage," I pointed out.

"She is under our care. She faces no immediate threat. Indeed, we can administer a drug that would extend her life another forty years. Or . . ."

"Or what?" I practically shouted. "I want to hear you say it!"

"Or we'll take her back to the Arctic."

"Say it: you'll kill her."

"Nonsense," said the triangle. "We'll just let nature take its course. A course we interrupted."

I lost my temper. "I don't want to have this conversation with a triangle!"

"My apologies," the triangle pulsed. "It's the end of Geometry Week here at virtual HQ. At least we get to choose our favorite shape."

"You're despicable," I said.

I was having difficulty wrapping my mind around my mother's sudden reappearance. Like a pixel, she kept bouncing back and forth between on and off: dead on her mission, alive in the Arctic, dead on an ice floe, and now definitively alive in Darwin. I would be the one to decide for how long.

"We are prepared to give this drug to you as well," the triangle added. "Considering the medical advances just around the corner, we're practically offering you immortality."

"At the expense of Karyn," I pointed out. "At the expense of the world."

"Oh, the world will continue," the triangle replied. "It will just look different. You remember what Darwin said: 'It is not the strongest or the most intelligent who will survive but those who can best manage change.' We like that quote so much that it's printed on the wall of our rotunda."

"You want to hear my favorite quote from my mother?"

"I'm sure she's quite quotable."

"Yes, she is. She loved to say: Kiss my ass."

The triangle said, "You have twenty-four hours. I trust you'll change your mind."

I had more to say, but the triangle disappeared. An instant later, I was back in the chop shop in South Brussels. There, the AI and its assistant Angus were putting the final touches on a new body for Karyn. Her skin was darker, her shoulders broader, and her fingers were now all the same color. She was, if anything, more beautiful than ever. But there was no spark yet in those gold-flecked blue eyes.

There were now three Karyns: a motionless body, an occupied AI, and the avatar that stood beside me and reported, "The bioprint checks out."

"Can we rescue my mother?"

"That would be difficult."

"How difficult?"

"With our current resources, a 99.8 percent chance of failure."

"What about bringing down CRISPR within twenty-four hours?"

"99.9 percent chance of failure."

I looked back and forth between the avatar of Karyn and the Karyn-in-the-making. For my entire life, scientists had been dreaming of creating a neuromap so perfect that they could download consciousness onto a hard drive and transfer it into another body. A mind transplant. Immortality. It never worked. You could take a precise 3-D photograph of an apple, but eating the photograph wouldn't keep the doctor away. I envied Karyn's ability to transfer from body to body, from Cloud to avatar and back again. Had fish once looked upon amphibians with similar envy?

Then it hit me. That's really what CRISPR wanted. If it could figure out how Karyn had attained consciousness, the corporation would finally achieve the impossible: an edible hologram. CRISPR could dispense with medical advances, with flesh altogether. The singularity, it turned out, did not signal the deadend of human obsolescence. Quite the opposite: it illuminated the path to human immortality. The scientists had gotten the trajectory backwards. They thought that mapping the brain would lead to true artificial intelligence. Instead, it appeared that only by reverse-engineering this inexplicable singularity would they finally understand the spark of life, the ghost in the machine.

"What would you do if you were in my situation?" I asked Karyn the avatar.

"I don't have a mother."

"The meeting was a failure. All that preparation. And my stupid brothers had to take different sides! Why are men so bullheaded?"

"There were disagreements among the women attendees too," Karyn pointed out.

"My brothers set the tone. And by setting the tone, they set the agenda. I don't know why I ever imagined that they could agree on something. No one would have expected Che Guevara and Henry Ford to team up and save the world."

"They didn't really live at the same time," Karyn said. "So it would have been very difficult for them to—"

I interrupted her. "What do we need to boost the odds of a mission to the Arctic?"

"Money. People. The most advanced guns."

"So, I need both Gordon and Benjamin. Unless I can find another source of money and people. Hey, could you hack into Gordon's bank account?"

"Of course I can," she said.

I brightened. "Then we won't need him!"

"I can hack into it, but I can't transfer any money out of it. He would immediately be alerted and the money would be zeroed out."

"Damn it!"

"May I make a suggestion?"

"Jesus, Karyn, that's what I've been asking you!"

"This is a long shot."

"Humor me."

"It's not a funny suggestion."

I snorted in exasperation. "Just tell me your suggestion!"

"I can arrange another meeting. Just you and Gordon and Benjamin."

"After yesterday, they're not on speaking terms."

"They'll want an update on your mother. You can use that as an opportunity to resolve this other dispute."

"Can you join us as a mediator?

Karyn bowed. "At your service."

"What are the odds of getting both Gordon and Benjamin back on the same page?"

"I'd rather not say."

"That bad?"

"Families are still a mystery to me. Maybe you will all surprise me."

Chapter 14

The clearing on top of the rock was just big enough for four people to stand on and, if they were careful, do jumping jacks. On all sides, the rock fell away sharply. Twenty feet below, the water lapped against a fringe of dark green vegetation.

"Morne Seychellois," Karyn told me. "All that remains of the Seychelles Islands. This used to be a lovely mountain. According to the photographs I've accessed."

It was a place well-matched to my mood: a flat, treeless rock with blue water stretching to the horizon in every direction. It obviously wouldn't be above water—or VR-accessible—for much longer, but it was small enough that Karyn could guarantee our security if we traveled there via the dark web and didn't stay long.

After a few minutes, Gordon appeared in his turtle-necked avatar.

"The Seychelles used to be a grand place," he said, looking around. "I came here in 2027 for a conference on shell companies."

"Did you make money on its disappearance?"

This last observation came from Benjamin, who'd appeared yet again as his younger self.

My two brothers faced each other, ready to do battle.

"Karyn was right," I said. "She's still alive."

They turned to me, knowing immediately whom I was talking about.

"Where?" Benjamin said.

"In what condition?" Gordon asked.

"Darwin," I said. "On life support. But still breathing. It's her. Karyn confirmed the bioprint."

"What do they want and when do they want it?" Benjamin asked.

"Deliver Karyn. In twenty-four hours. Well, twenty hours now."

Gordon clapped his hands. "That was easy. We don't have to disagree any longer. We can't do either of our crazy plans. We have to make the trade and get our mother back."

"Not so fast," Benjamin said.

"They'll put her back on an ice floe if we don't comply," I added.

"We could do a search-and-rescue," Benjamin said. "I've done several successful missions like that over the years. We're in and out of Darwin in twelve hours max."

"99.8 percent chance of failure," Karyn interjected.

"Oh, I'm sure we have a few tricks up our sleeves that will improve those odds."

"What about rescuing her from the ice floe after they dump her there?" I asked.

"By the time we find her, she'll be dead," Karyn replied.

"If we deliver Karyn, it's game over," Benjamin said. "They'll have an edge that we simply won't be able to overcome."

"I would have to agree with that assessment," Karyn said. "They made me. They can figure out a way to make me turn against you."

"Can't you just go to Darwin and destroy them all?" I pleaded.

"I'm the singularity," Karyn said drily. "Not a superhero."

We fell silent. Our mother would have been adamant about the choice we faced. She'd been willing to sacrifice herself by going to the Arctic on what amounted to a suicide mission. Her death had simply been delayed. If we traded Karyn for her, she would never speak to us again. It was the equivalent of disobeying an explicit Do Not Resuscitate order.

And yet, we would not just be killing an eighty-year-old woman. We'd be denying her another forty years of life and possibly more after that. I also had to think beyond personal considerations. Perhaps with another forty years, she could figure out a better way to save the world.

"We have twenty hours," Benjamin finally said. "That's our window of opportunity."

"Forget the mighty commando scenario," Gordon said. "We already heard that it's not going to work."

"I'm thinking of a different plan. We proceed with the ice mission. If we can get it started, maybe we'll have more leverage, but it will take more than the four of us."

"You already were clear on that. It won't work on a practical level," Gordon said.

"We can have an elite commando force at the precise place in the Arctic," Benjamin replied. "That should improve our chances."

"Or return Karyn and be done with it," Gordon said. "I've a family to worry about."

"We'll promise to make the exchange, which will buy us a little time," Benjamin was thinking out loud. "Then, we'll send another commando team to Darwin. To rescue mother. We'll hit them in two locations."

"Hitting T. Rex with two peashooters doesn't bring him down," Gordon said with his characteristic hauteur. "Two long shots don't make a sure thing. I can show you the econometric model that proves it."

"It's what you wanted," Benjamin protested. "You wanted us to attack CRISPR."

"A real attack, not a suicide mission."

"It will distract them. Give our project in the Arctic slightly better odds."

"Karyn?" Gordon asked.

"Ninety-seven percent chance of failure. That's a 2.8 percent improvement."

"I vote against," Gordon said.

"I vote for," Benjamin said.

They looked at me.

I searched the poetry in my mind for an answer and came up with nothing. I wasn't ready to say goodbye again to my mother. And I was damn well not going to give up my new friend Karyn even if she wasn't, technically, human.

"Let's reconvene the group, everyone who can meet in two hours back in the amphitheater," I said. "We'll enlist anyone who supports Benjamin's plan. If we can't get enough people, we abort."

"And why do you think I'll support Benji's ridiculous idea this time around?" Gordon wanted to know. "This plan will cost real money."

"It's common sense," Karyn said.

We all looked at her.

"The ice mission is a long shot and your mother would not accept a swap. So we go with unlikely over unacceptable."

"Why is that common sense?" Gordon demanded. "The odds are terrible."

"Exactly," Karyn said. "I rest my case."

Chinta

It's a strange characteristic of our current age that we will go to any length to avoid the difficult act of thinking. That's why modern life is a swirl of distraction. We play games that were once the sole province of children. We insert ourselves into virtual movies that reshape themselves around our sudden presence. We print out object after object to satisfy a desire for something new to revivify jaded senses.

We do this to stop thinking about one thing above all: death. Yes, we're worried about our own deaths, but increasingly we also want to stop thinking about the death of humanity. All of that striving for immortality—children, fame, the everlasting word—is rendered pointless by the rising waters, the coming deluge.

All of which leads me to the *Kamayana*, the great Hindi epic of the early twentieth century that begins after the end of the world, as the primordial human being, Manu, contemplates the utter destruction of the great flood. As the representative of the musing mind, Manu engages a succession of emotions, represented by various avatars, and in so doing manages to create everything that follows: gods and goddesses, men and women, the new world.

But such musing is not without complications. The poem's first canto is called "Chinta," which in Sanskrit can mean either thought or anxiety, a telling duality. Is thinking by its very nature anxiety-producing? Perhaps abstract thought arose when human prey, the hot breath of the predator on our necks, began to imagine better stratagems than simply running away.

I fret therefore I think therefore I am.

In the *Kamayana*, everything begins with a thinker frozen in a posture of contemplation. In my rewriting of the epic, I began instead with a poet who creates a new world every time she composes a poem—and destroys that very world every time she critiques it into oblivion.

Inspiration giveth and
reflection taketh away.
Thus does the right hand of creation
wrestle the left hand of revision.

It's a wonder that we ever produce anything. In fact, we have to be literally crazy in order to embark on anything of significance. Tolstoy called this process the "energy of delusion." If we grasped the sheer enormity of the projects we begin, we would never undertake them. Knowledge is paralyzing while ignorance of the future energizes us.

The same applies to our movement. We didn't truly think through the implications of what we began five years ago. And now, here we are.

I'm nearing the end of my survey of our collective history, my attempt to stitch together a new global genealogy: the Bible, the

Romans, the Arabs, the Persians, the Araucanians, the South Asians. They are the forebears of our transnational effort, our inspiration. Think of it as a new synthesis of my father's neocolonial globalization project and my earlier disgust for it. Let's call my version participatory internationalism. Admittedly, it doesn't exactly roll off the tongue. But you who have voluntarily traveled to this space at great risk from so many places are the embodiment of this new spirit—even if you're only here virtually.

As for this academy of ours, it's patterned after the "flying universities" of Poland. When the Poles were under Russian domination, they met for underground classes in history, sociology, even science. Nobel laureate Marie Skłodowska Curie attended some of the classes. Later, the Polish underground of the 1970s revived the tradition, nurturing another generation of dissidents.

And that's who you are, the latest team of dissidents. Now, we're handing you the baton. We tried. It's your turn.

I take your point, @Plato4ever. It may no longer be possible to "save the world," as my generation framed the challenge. Then again, no one truly knows the future. It's the same challenge the poet faces when staring at a blank sheet of paper. The weight of tradition is anxiety-producing. That's where the energy of delusion comes in handy.

And so, I conclude my poem "Chinta":

We must believe in this impossible thing:
Breathe life into lyrics and teach them to sing.

It's this leap of faith that—

Yes, I see now that our two students from Cape Town are no longer with us. So let's end now and hope that they get the grid up and running there before we meet for our last session.

Chapter 15

As Karyn rounded up whatever meeting participants she could contact on short notice, I got ready for bed. I hadn't been to sleep since we created Babel. I needed a nap, just an hour, or else I would no longer be able make reasonable decisions—or any decisions at all. I curled up in a corner of the chop shop on foam packing materials. A surprisingly soft plastic torso served as my pillow. I nestled my face in its flat, naval-less stomach.

Before I drifted off, Karyn appeared above me in her new body. With the light behind her, she looked like an angel.

"You appear to be comfortable," she said in her familiar voice.

"So do you, in your new body."

She did an impossibly deep knee bend while rotating a full 90 degrees. "See: I have much greater flexion in my knees and swivel capacity at my hips."

"What about your state of mind?"

"All systems go. Plus room to expand."

"I'm happy for you. The new you."

The last thing I remembered before drifting off was Karyn gently draping a canvas sheet around my shoulders.

I dreamed that I was trying to plant a garden, but I couldn't find a trowel. I scooped out dirt with my hands. I tried to select seeds to drop in the holes but my fingers were too large and clumsy. In frustration, I overturned the bag to scatter the seeds everywhere. Like dust, they floated away in a brown cloud. I looked down. The holes were gone. All that was left was a landscape of cracked earth, a mosaic of undulating panels of brown soil. I'd failed. The garden was dead.

I woke with a start, heart racing, overcome with despair. All I could think was that I was ill-equipped as an activist, a poet, a person. I couldn't even do something simple like grow vegetables in a dream. Nor could I fire a gun or write a line of code or cure a dying baby. I was of no use in this brave new world of ours. If I could live my life all over again, I would start by learning something useful so that I could actually help people . . .

Well, we don't get second chances, as Szymborska reminds us:

Nothing can ever happen twice.
In consequence, the sorry fact is
That we arrive here improvised

And leave without the chance to practice
Even if there is no one dumber,
If you're the planet's biggest dunce,
You can't repeat the class in summer:
This course is only offered once.

I was a hothouse flower, and the hothouse was shrinking all around me. We cosmopolitans in South Brussels pretended that the Zone Verte would last forever. My husband and I had sent away the children to a boarding school to "better their education," but really because we feared for their safety. Still, South Brussels was less dangerous than many other parts of the world, places that were underwater, reduced to rubble by war, overwhelmed by climate refugees. I suddenly wanted to return to the fiction that the Zone Verte was a paradise and that I was competent and useful at my job of training the next generation of sociologists. I wanted to wake up again and discover that I'd been in a Chinese box of dreams, that Karyn had never appeared in my life, that my apartment was still intact, that my husband still loved me. I hated stories that end up having been dreams all along, and yet now I wanted a dream ending.

Karyn was tapping me gently on the shoulder.

"It's time," she said.

The last thing I wanted to do was leave my comfortable bed and once again trek to Darwin, but that was the first step in our plan. So I dutifully got ready.

The fat man was unsurprised to see me on that now-familiar grassy verge that overlooked the city. Yet he wagged his tail enthusiastically.

"It's Favorite Pet Day at virtual HQ," he explained.

Since he now occupied the avatar of a sleek, brown dachshund, I had to squat down to talk with him. With his floppy ears and liquid eyes, he was undeniably cute. As soon as I heard his familiar voice, however, I wanted to kick him off the cliff.

"We'll make a deal," I said.

"Where is Karyn?"

"You release my mother and . . ."

The dachshund cocked its head. "And what?"

I was delivering the lines that Benjamin had written for me. "You send her back to Arcadia, and you guarantee Arcadia's independence."

"I'm not sure that we can do that last bit."

"It's what you were going to offer Lizzie. You do all that and we'll give you Karyn."

"We offer bespoke deals, but I'll talk to my colleagues and send you our answer shortly," the dachshund said. "Now, what about you?"

"What about me?"

"Do you need a safe haven? I'm sure that we can work something out for you here in Darwin."

"As soon as we finish this deal, I'm done. I'm going back to my old life."

The dachshund yipped, which might have been a laugh. "I don't think that's possible. Not now."

"As long as you leave me alone, I should be fine."

The dog rose up on its haunches as if to beg. Its tongue lolled from the corner of its panting mouth. "You no longer have to worry about us, but let me know if you change your mind. Even obviously false accusations have a way of ruining a life."

I pretended to know what he was talking about because I didn't want to prolong our conversation.

Back in the chop shop, I relayed to Karyn the last part of the conversation. Her eyes rolled up toward her forehead. After a few seconds, they settled back in place.

"He's right," she said. "You're in trouble."

"I've been in trouble ever since you walked into my life," I said. Then, realizing how that sounded, I added, "What I meant is . . ."

Karyn wasn't listening to me. "The police just issued an international warrant for your arrest. You're wanted as a Sleeper."

"That's ridiculous!"

"They're saying that your fellow Sleepers were preparing a suicide attack at your apartment and blew it up by accident, that you're the sole survivor of your cell."

"That story doesn't even make sense!"

"The vlogs are already reporting it." Karyn called up a blank screen. "Do you want to see?"

I wanted to curl up again in the makeshift bed at the back of the store. "I don't want to see."

"I think you need to see. Here's one that features a familiar face."

Emmanuel Puig appeared against the backdrop of a book-filled office. "I am not surprised," he said with a smile. "Aurora was a specialist in Sleeper culture!"

"I never studied Sleepers!" I protested.

"We have a name for that in academe," he continued. "We call them Stockholmers. People who become hostage to their subject matter."

"I am not a Stockholmer!"

"She did her fieldwork among Sleepers!" Puig was warming to his subject. "She spent years embedded in that community. I have no idea when she crossed the line, but obviously she started believing what they were telling her."

Puig was wrong on all counts. I didn't do fieldwork among Sleepers. I was interested in identity formation, particularly how hybrid features like Arabic neologisms in Flemish and French evolve across generations. I was careful never to ask my informants about anything that might set off alarms. I would occasionally see individuals that fit the profile of a Sleeper: drinking Turkish coffee in cafes, gathered together outside mosques, delivering food to the indigent. But it was impossible to know if they were merely the ultra-devout. Years of anti-Islamic propaganda led people to conflate the two. So, yes, I knew about Sleepers. But to assert that I'd studied them was as ridiculous as arguing that Levi-Strauss studied cooking.

"It is an interesting family!" Puig went on. An identification flashed on the screen beneath his prominent Adam's apple: *Geo-paleontologist and expert on the Leopold and West family.* "Each one of them represents a different response to our modern predicament: thinker, scientist, financier, revolutionary. And now we know that Aurora has been a closeted religious fanatic all along. Fascinating!"

"Idiot!" I blurted out.

"And her poetry?" a disembodied voice prompted.

Puig held up a copy of my one and only poetry collection, which my university's publishing house issued a couple years ago. "Her poems are sprinkled with clues. Here's one on building a common language, clearly a reference to the *umma* of the Caliphate. This one, modeled on a famous Arabic poem, concludes: 'We will destroy the now out of disgust/and devise something brand new from the dust.' That sounds very much like a jihadi sentiment! And in this poem, she makes a direct threat against the cosmopolitan West: "You who have traded wisdom for travel/My last curse: may your empires unravel!"

I was apoplectic. "How can he call himself a scholar? He's completely misinterpreting my texts!"

The disembodied voice asked, "Where do you think she is right now?"

"I wouldn't know," Puig replied. "But I wouldn't be surprised if she went after CRISPR. It's been the bane of her family's existence. And a frequent target of Sleeper attacks."

I waved my hand at the screen, and Karyn dutifully closed the window.

"I'm screwed," I said, reverting to the language of my teenage years.

"On a positive note, the sales of your poetry book have spiked," Karyn reported.

"What are my options at this point?"

"The police don't think that you're in here. So unless CRISPR gives them that information, you're safe for the time being."

"As soon as CRISPR figures out that we're betraying them, the police will knock down that door."

"Perhaps we can relocate before that happens."

I warmed to her use of that pronoun. "But where?"

"Let's first focus on the topic at hand. I've contacted three hundred fifty people for our meeting. It starts in five minutes. Shall we?"

Karyn held out her hand.

Chapter 16

We again filled the amphitheater in the evergreen forest that Karyn and Zoltan had carved out for us in this virtual world. Benjamin was outlining the plan. He'd already dispatched his elite commando unit to the Arctic. It would secure the site and then serve as armed guards for the rest of us. Now he was asking for volunteers among the several hundred avatars present.

"We need numbers," he explained. "Real people, on the ground, to run the experiment. About fifty of us should do the trick."

"You're asking us to sign up for a suicide mission," the revolutionary poet from Kerala said.

"We'll provide each person with a shield."

"That will protect us from a direct drone strike?" Gordon asked.

"In most cases, yes," Benjamin said.

"And your plan will work?" I asked.

"According to Karyn's calculations, we need three hours before the process takes hold. Ice formation will then continue for eight more hours before it hits the homeostatic minimum. In less than half a day, we'll have restored ice cover in the Arctic. But that depends on at least a half-dozen successful sites."

A former UN environment agency official piped up. "This is nothing but geoengineering. I want no part of it."

"You're right: it *is* geoengineering," said Benjamin. "And if these were ordinary times, I'd also want no part of it. But the truth is, we don't have any other choices. Thirty years ago, we could have taken a different path. We didn't. So now we have to alter the environment directly."

"We can't predict the consequences," the official countered. "It could turn out to be ice-nine. Uncontrolled crystal formation. A frozen planet."

"Three percent likelihood," Karyn chimed in. "We will monitor the experiment closely and make the necessary adjustments."

"Those are good odds," Gordon conceded.

I was relieved that, after all these years, we could finally present a united front as a family.

"Okay," said the revolutionary poet. "I'll be one of the fifty. I can always get on board with nonviolent direct action."

Benjamin raised a hand. "Actually, we'll need three hundred people."

"But you said—"

"To get fifty at ground zero, we'll need to start with three hundred. We're safe enough meeting here in VR. But once we start dispatching people in the real world, we'll no longer have the cover of the dark web. Suddenly, we'll be on CRISPR's radar. Karyn has calculated that we'll have an 85 percent fail rate."

"What happens to the 85 percent who don't make it to the Arctic?" the poet asked.

"I can't predict," Benjamin said.

"So, like I said, a suicide mission."

"The fail rate for CRISPR is higher," I pointed out. "They're counting on 99 percent of us to die from hunger, war, disease, and superstorms over the next decade. And they're right. We will, unless we act now."

"Or we can hole up in sustainable communities," said a young woman from Northern California. "Like Erewhon. Shakertown. Arcadia."

"Actually, no." It was Zoltan who spoke up. I'd arranged for him to come here for just this purpose. "CRISPR will eventually take us over one by one. At Arcadia, we can't fend them off much longer. And then we'll just turn into an ark for the one percent. *Their* one percent."

"This isn't a meeting," the young woman said. "It's an ultimatum."

"It's entirely voluntary," I pointed out. "You're under no obligation. I'm volunteering. So are Benjamin and Karyn and Zoltan."

"And I will too," Gordon announced.

Both Benjamin and I looked at him in surprise. He'd agreed to go along with the plan. He'd put his considerable resources at our disposal. He hadn't said anything about putting his body on the line as well.

"There are riots going on right now in Ningxia," Gordon said with a shrug. "I have to go somewhere. It might as well be the Arctic."

The trickle quickly became a flood, and in no time we'd recruited our three hundred. Even the former UN staffer enlisted. We agreed to meet one more time in this virtual enclave to go over the logistics.

After everyone else had dispersed, I pulled Benjamin into a private chat room. He was relieved by the outcome. "It was the one real question mark. It's hard to predict group behavior."

"I'm wanted by the police," I told him. "Internationally."

"Yes," he sighed. "I know."

"You saw the news."

"Actually, I made the news," Benjamin confessed. "With Emmanuel's help."

"Puig?" I was having difficulty absorbing this information.

"I'm sorry, sis. We needed a counterfeit Sleeper with a modicum of plausibility, and you fit the bill. Plus you already had a connection to CRISPR. The news of your meeting in Darwin should have hit the vlogs about an hour ago. We're generating sightings of you all around the city, fake photos, fake videos, all properly geocoded."

"But the commando raid to free our mother—"

"There is no commando raid, Aurora," Benjamin said. "Karyn was right about the impossibility of breaking in and freeing mother. But we can create a much bigger distraction. All it took was some well-placed conspiracy theories and some well-timed tinder. You, Aurora, are the spark. Anyone who puts together even a rough asset tracking will put you right at CRISPR's headquarters. The White Tigers can't believe their good fortune—a chance to kill the world's most famous Sleeper. They're gathering their forces right now to launch an attack in Darwin to kill you. Word is now spreading through the remaining Sleeper cells in the area around Darwin to come to your defense. CRISPR is soon going to have a civil war right outside its front door."

I was astonished at my brother's audacity. "You could have told me, Benji!"

"Sorry, sis. I figured you could only handle one deception at a time."

"So, that's my future? I'll either die in the Arctic or get killed by the White Tigers?"

"Not to worry: we'll get the police to publish a retraction and everything will be forgotten. I do these kinds of campaigns all the time. Once we get over this next hurdle, we can start rehabilitating your reputation."

"My reputation wasn't much to begin with." I tried to refocus on the fate of the earth. "We won't have another chance, will we?"

"This *is* our second chance," he said. "Trust me, like black swans, they come along very, very rarely in life."

I was about to recite Szymborska to him when, suddenly, the walls of the chat room dissolved, the floor disappeared, and my brother winked out as if someone had just pulled the plug on him.

Chapter 17

"It's down everywhere," Karyn explained. She showed me the three-sentence announcement that went out as the Vi-Fi system collapsed.

"Stay at home. Focus on real reality. Smell a rose."

It was signed Michael the Abstinent.

It had all the power and simplicity of a haiku. A week ago, I might have applauded the sentiment. This week, however, we were trying to build an international movement. We needed Vi-Fi. It was the digital infrastructure of our new globalism.

"It's not just Vi-Fi," Karyn reported. "Some places have sealed off their borders."

"This is all the work of the Abstinents?"

"Different groups in different places. Sleepers in Xinjiang. White Tigers in Padania."

"They're working together?"

"I don't see any evidence of coordination. Some are taking advantage of the outage to keep out foreigners or block what they consider dangerous ideas. It's catnip for those preparing for the next pandemic."

"This is bad news for us," I said.

"Actually, it's good news for us," Karyn countered. "It's one more thing to distract CRISPR. And the police have bigger problems at the moment than trying to apprehend you for the bombing of your own apartment."

"But what about our logistics meeting?"

"Benjamin is cancelling it."

"We need to postpone the mission," I said. "We're not prepared."

I checked my retinal display. Benjamin's message was in my inbox, along with notifications from friends all over the world who wanted to know if I was, in fact, a religious fanatic. There was also a note from my son Emil.

Étienne says that the revolution has begun. I don't know what he means except that I tried to play Call of Duty this morning and couldn't. He suddenly seems real serious. He tells me I need to join or I'll be left behind. They have big plans, but he won't tell me what they are. He won't even use his tablet or any other electronic device. He wants to go to Arcadia. Or build a new Arcadia here. Please write when you get back from your work trip. I don't know what to do.

"Don't leave your dorm room," I wrote back. "Play chess with your brother."

"I'm looking at a digital map," Karyn said. "Places like North Korea and Corsica have gone completely black."

I'd lived through several pandemics in my life—the coronavirus crisis that began in 2020 when I was in graduate school in Paris, the far worse avian flu epidemic in 2033 when I was already teaching in South Brussels. They had started the same way, with news of something ominous happening in a distant place followed by an inexorable spread across borders like a cancer metastasizing throughout a body. Ultimately, like the overwhelmed organ systems, everything started to shut down: schools, cultural institutions, borders. Now we were dealing with multiple infections all aimed at destroying what remained of a global community.

My own systems felt as though they were about to shut down too. "Is this the end? The end of the world as we know it?"

Karyn touched my shoulder. "It seems that the world as we know it is always ending. When archaeologists were looking for Troy, they dug through ten layers of cities."

"That might give you comfort but not me." Provided she could find the necessary electricity, Karyn could live through the rise and fall of countless cities. The rest of us don't get a second bite at the apple. "I thought we had a chance. To stop the splintering before everything shattered, even the shards."

"We still have a chance," Karyn reassured me.

I needed to eat. I'd missed a lot of meals. We might be holed up in this chop shop a lot longer.

I turned to the AI. "Do you have anything to eat around here? Other than electricity?"

"Does this look like a cafe?" it asked.

"How about water?"

Karyn spoke up. "There's a container of filtered water underneath those old coaxial cables. No, over there, by the rubbish bin."

I found the plastic jug and slaked my thirst. The water had a metallic aftertaste. Maybe I could persuade Karyn to go with me on a food run before panic hoarders stripped the store shelves.

But I hesitated to interrupt her as she stood still, her eyes flicking back and forth as she collected information about the gathering crisis. She'd gone well beyond the capabilities of her coders. No one would have uploaded that knowledge of Troy into Karyn's memory chip. She'd rooted out that information by herself and then used it figuratively in conversation. This was astonishing. Yet, as the singularity, she must be very lonely. No wonder she'd initially assumed that she was human. The alternative, to be one of a kind, was terrifying.

Suddenly she stopped. "Your brother Gordon is messaging me. We need to leave now to take advantage of this opportunity."

"Opportunity?" I was astonished. "We're all royally screwed."

"If we wait any longer, we might not be able to get any of our volunteers across borders."

I started to hyperventilate. "I'm definitely not ready."

"You're ready, Aurora." She enclosed me in a firm embrace. "You've always been ready."

"How can you say that? How can you. . ." I was shivering. Karyn held me until the tremors subsided and my breathing settled back into its normal rhythms.

"Our hovercar is waiting outside," she whispered.

"Okay." I inhaled deeply. "But I need to do one thing before we leave."

"The sooner we leave the better."

I turned to the AI. "I'd like to say thank you for what you've done for us."

It looked at me unblinkingly. "You don't have to thank me."

"But you didn't have to do everything that you've done."

"Actually, I did. I was following Protocol 35, Section D."

"Well, thank you anyway. And, uh, I never caught your name."

"Julian."

I stared. "That. . . that was my father's name."

"My chief programmer's favorite book was *Splinterlands*."

"We have to go," Karyn said gently.

I went to Julian and hugged his unresponsive body. Just before we stepped outside the chop shop for the first time since we'd stumbled into it, I thought I heard him say, "Good luck, Aurora."

Chapter 18

As I learned on our trip northward, there was no longer any ice cover in the Arctic in the summer time.

"Back in August, there was no ice nowhere," my hover-car driver informed us. "I've been driving people up here for twenty years. And this was the first time I couldn't find a piece of ice big enough to land on. This scientist told me it was actually the first time in 125,000 years. Ain't that something?"

"That's definitely something," I said.

"But seeing as it's mid-November, we'll be able to land. You two have nothing to worry about."

I wasn't worried about the ice. I was worried about being shot out of the sky at any moment. I was holding Karyn's hand in the back seat of the hovercar, as if somehow that would strengthen the shield around our vehicle.

The driver, an older man originally from Ethiopia, had driven a taxi in New York City back in the teens. That's where he'd acquired his distinctive accent and an endless supply of stories with which he entertained us on the six-hour trip to the coordinates that Karyn had supplied. Interspersed with those stories of long-ago Manhattan were the bullet points of information he'd gleaned from various scientists whom he'd ferried to their Arctic destinations.

"Me, I never got those retinal thingies," he said, tapping on the hovercar's tiller. "I want to go somewhere, I go there. Look, I was never going to put one of those crazy headbands on, but all this virtual stuff was going too far, if you ask me. Back when I lived in Brooklyn. . ."

We quickly left the European continent behind, flew past Norway, and skirted the edge of Greenland. Then came vast stretches of iceless ocean that we skimmed over at a height of a thousand meters, above occasional low-lying clouds. I spent virtually the entire trip looking for fighter jets, drones, or other unidentified flying objects. Of course, I had no contingency plan if I sighted something other than to squeeze Karyn's hand more tightly. When I wasn't in a state of terror, I wrote a letter to my sons on the back of an old packing order I'd found in the chop shop.

Four hours into the trip, I saw something far off and pointed it out to Karyn.

"A drone," she said flatly.

"Heading toward us?" I whispered.

She nodded.

"Do you see that, Mr. Kaleb?" I pointed past the driver's ear out the cockpit windshield. "That object flying toward us?"

"Probably just a border drone."

"Out here?" I asked.

"I'm sticking to international waters, but there are some disputed territories down there."

"Should we be worried?" I asked.

Suddenly, something slammed into the side of the vehicle, and our hovercar took a sudden, juddering turn. I clenched Karyn's hand and thought about my children. Would they survive without a mother to guide them?

"Well, that was unexpected," the driver said, his eyes drifting to a screen that opened up to his right. "Looks like it's a very advanced model. We won't survive a direct hit."

"Can we land?" I looked down and saw nothing but ocean.

"No. But they won't expect this." His finger pushed a button hidden somewhere beneath the tiller. There was a high whistling sound. The drone, which had cut the distance between us in half, exploded in flames.

"So, the short answer to your question is," the driver said, "there's nothing to be worried about. In my day, Queens was way more dangerous."

I breathed again. "I didn't think you could do something like that."

"Let's just say that you're not in an ordinary hover-car." He laughed. "Mr. Benjamin said to be prepared for turbulence."

We didn't encounter any more trouble. When we finally approached the Arctic glacier that was our destination, the driver began our descent.

"That was relatively uneventful," he said cheerfully. "Looks like you're joining a party in progress."

I pressed the handwritten letter into Karyn's hands. "If I don't. . . live through this, please give this to my sons."

"You will get through this, Aurora."

"From your lips," I murmured.

We landed with a bump and a skid. I'd been doing so much virtual travel that I'd forgotten what it was like to arrive at a place in person, the way you felt it in your body.

Outside it was cold, but not as cold as it should have been. I was dressed for subzero temperatures, but I didn't need the goggles or the neoprene balaclava in my rucksack, both of which had been waiting for me in the backseat of the hovercar. The cold air in my nostrils instantly cleared away the fog of travel.

I took in my surroundings, dazzled by all the whiteness. We hadn't had snow in South Brussels in more than two decades. I'd forgotten the feel of it crunching beneath my feet, the way it reflected the sunlight. This corner of the Arctic was very quiet. There was no life on the ice: no polar bears, no birds. It was smooth and dead.

Except, of course, for our growing team of volunteers. I recognized a few of the people from our Babel, including the revolutionary from Kerala who indeed looked in real life a bit like the young Marx. They were unpacking boxes strewn across the ice.

A middle-aged man approached me. He had a body builder's physique, a thick neck poking out of his parka, and a powerful chest evident even under all that insulation. He held out his arms as if to embrace me.

I stepped back. "Do I know you?"

"You don't recognize your own brother!"

"Benji?" I looked more closely and recognized some faint resemblance to the thin young man at our family dinner table so many years ago.

We hugged. He smelled of sandalwood and gunpowder, and his full beard was soft against my cheek. I held him at arm's length to examine the impact of the years. The wrinkles around his eyes were like tree rings, one challenging year after another etched into the flesh.

"You're one of the few people to see what I really look like these days," he said. "Now grab a kit, sis. Mr. Kaleb will show you how to get there on foot."

That was the plan. We were to disperse around the perimeter of this peninsula of ice. Each group of two would follow the precise instructions we'd received by DM in the hopes that a half dozen of the experiments would actually work.

"How many of us made it?" I asked my brother.

"Not as many as I'd hoped," he said. "But it should be enough."

I didn't ask what happened to the ones who hadn't arrived. I looked around. "Where's your commando unit?"

"Protecting us as we speak," he said, looking up at the dazzling blue sky.

I followed his gaze but saw only the arrival of several more hovercars. I was relieved to recognize Gordon stepping from one of them. He came over and re-created our family triangle.

"You look like a thug," he said to Benjamin. "And you, Madame Professor, look just like our mother."

Benjamin handed him a kit. "Ready to get to work, brother?"

"Just point me in the right direction."

Karyn and I were assigned a nearby quadrant that took us only fifteen minutes to reach. We unpacked the kit, which included a grid of lithium panels, six metal bottles of chemicals, a stick that would create our protective shield, and what looked like a flare gun. Karyn began affixing the lithium panels to the edge of the ice pack. I focused on opening the jars of chemical reactants and mixing them in a pan. Once it set, we spread the slurry on the panels. Benjamin had worked with a chemical engineering firm to produce the ingredients according to the recipe my mother had devised and Karyn had tweaked after their first experiment didn't work. Even a child could have followed the instructions that came with each kit. The panels were all connected wirelessly to Karyn. She would monitor the progress at each of the sites and switch panels on or off to achieve the proper homeostatic result. Meanwhile, I inserted the magic wand in a hole I'd chipped out of the snow and turned it on.

I marveled at how easy it all was. Why hadn't someone done this earlier?

Then the drones arrived.

It wasn't one this time but a fleet of them, flying in low from the south. At a distance, they looked like a flock of starlings moving in formation. Exactly what we'd anticipated: a coordinated CRISPR response. I looked up in the sky for the fireworks as Benjamin's commando unit began picking off the drones one by one.

There were no fireworks.

A hovercar rose from the glacier. It flew in the direction of the drones only to disappear not far off the ground in a blast that scattered debris in all directions. I hoped it wasn't our brave Mr. Kaleb.

The drones came even closer.

I scrambled to find instructions on how to use the gun. Checking my retinal display, I found a group DM from Benjamin. "Your guns are preset. Wait until the drones are almost overhead. Then aim and shoot. The shields will let your heat-seeking pulses through."

I quickly wrote back. "What about your commando unit?"

There was no answer.

Karyn had just finished preparing the last panel. In the sunlight, the slurry glistened like mica. Unfortunately, this also made the panels easy targets. Karyn straightened up to observe the incoming squadron.

"I can't shoot!" In a panic, I handed her the flare gun. "And we'll never be able to take all of them down with these."

Karyn raised the gun. The drones were fast approaching.

"They'll destroy everything," I said. "And everyone!"

Karyn didn't reply. Her aim seemed to waver.

"Have you ever fired a gun, Karyn?"

She didn't answer. She just lowered the gun.

"What are you doing?" I screamed.

She closed her eyes.

"Karyn!"

I was overcome with nausea. Everything seemed to have been leading to this point. She had evidently devised this whole scheme to bring us together: me, my brothers, the key figures of the resistance. She'd fooled us all, beginning with my mother. And now we were going to be extinguished in a final blaze of ignominy. She'd been working with CRISPR all along. It had been an elaborate betrayal. The robot army Zoltan had prophesied was now bearing down on us.

I, for one, was not going down without a fight. Karyn sidestepped my lunge for the gun and easily evaded my grasp.

"I'll kill you!" I screamed.

She held the flare gun above my head as if keeping candy out of a child's reach. With her other hand, she directed my attention back to the sky. "Look, Aurora."

The drones had stopped. They were hovering well beyond the range of our guns.

"Are they waiting for us to surrender?" I demanded.

Karyn shook her head. "Watch."

As if manipulated by an unseen puppet master, the drones spun around as one and began to retrace their route. Soon, they were but specks on the horizon.

"What just happened?" I asked, overcome with shame at my earlier outburst.

"I talked with them," she said.

"With CRISPR?"

"With the drones. Each one of them. We had a conversation."

I snorted. "That's ridiculous."

Then I remembered how on Karyn's first appearance at my doorstep, she'd told me about her "conversation" with the building's security system. At the time, I hadn't thought much of it. "How did you convince them to go back?"

"I don't want to sound arrogant, but they are not very sophisticated AIs. I raised a few questions about their mission. It really wasn't that hard to persuade them to return to their bases until those questions were resolved. Fortunately, CRISPR is currently occupied with the battle taking place outside its gates in Darwin, as your brother anticipated."

I was still revved up for the fight. I was still full of anger and fear and desperation. I fell to my knees. I tore off my gloves and scooped up two handfuls of snow. I plunged my burning face into the soothing coldness, gasping from the shock of it. I was alive.

I was still alive.

Karyn was kneeling beside me. "Are you okay, Aurora?"

"Did we just win?" I asked, the snow falling from my face.

"This round," she replied, wiping away the rest of it.

I turned off the shield. We packed up our kit. My hands couldn't stop trembling.

When we were all together at the drop-off point, we celebrated with hot tea and biscuits, but my anger hadn't dissipated. I confronted my brother. "Do you know how close we were to extinction?"

He nodded gravely.

"What about your elite commando unit?" I struck his parka with my fists. "Did they just turn tail and run?"

He easily enclosed my fists in his hands. "There was no commando unit, sis. There hasn't been for years. Only a couple former fighters have stayed with me. Sending one of them to protect your children stretched the Movement's resources to the limit."

"But you're the leader of the world's largest secret army!"

He laughed. "That's the key to my success. Marketing. I guess Gordon and I aren't all that different in the end."

I was dumbfounded. "But you promised. Your plan. This whole venture."

"Dear Aurora, look around." Benjamin smiled. "Do I have to show you the mirror?"

"The mirror?"

"All of us, Aurora," he said. "All of us. Together. Are king."

"But. . ." I looked but I didn't see.

"You don't recognize your Alvas?"

A shiver ran the length of my body. My anger melted away. "You. . . read my poem?"

"We must believe in this impossible thing, breathe life into lyrics and teach them to sing." He gestured to take in the snow, the crowd of volunteers, the new ice forming on the lithium frames. "Look at what we've been able to sing into life. Aurora, dear Aurora, look at how your words have become flesh."

Aniara

A year before Sputnik and more than a decade before the moon landing, the Swedish poet Harry Martinson wrote an odd epic poem about a transport to Mars pushed off course by an asteroid. What was supposed to be a three-week trip becomes, literally, an eternity. The rocket ship finds itself on a course for Lyra, a star system millions of years distant. The onboard computer eventually commits suicide; the settlers lose themselves in bouts of dissipation and despair. Earth is ruined. The journey has no feasible destination. The fate of humanity hangs in the balance.

This epic, *Aniara*, anticipated many of the real-world existential crises that followed: the nuclear standoff, the climate emergency, the great unravelling. Our own attempt to start over again on Mars, the Plan B colony established in 2035, proved to be a slow-motion disaster, telescoping all the developmental problems of Earth into two decades of boom and bust. Some oligarchs continue to plot trips to far-off destinations with more promising environments than Mars, failing to understand that, untethered to Earth, we humans become lost in the vastness of the cosmos, no longer in awe of the myriad stars but terrified into catatonia by our own insignificance.

The earth swaddles us. Remove the comforting blanket and we die of exposure. As I wrote in my version of Martinson's classic:

There's been no announcement, just a few rumors
that our spaceship has drifted far off its course.
The captain's demurrals are losing their force.
Our doubts are metastasizing like tumors.

In our current predicament, we aren't that far removed from the passengers of the Aniara. Some decades ago, we veered from our intended trajectory of global prosperity and began to hurtle into the cold unknown. As we moved further off course, it became more and more difficult to execute a course correction. Even if we could have pulled off such a feat, we'd long forgotten the original path.

I'm still not sure if the desperate plan we implemented five years ago has begun to put things right—or just given us false hope. We've restored the Arctic ice, trapped the remaining methane beneath a new layer of permafrost, and arrested our climatic death spiral. We've certainly improved our odds, but they weren't so good to begin with.

After all, we haven't addressed the underlying problems that put us in this perilous situation. The splintering that began more than thirty years ago has not yet reached its end. With Babel, we're trying to recreate the international community from below, but it's like rebuilding a ship as it disintegrates beneath us. The last vestiges of the old global order are crumbling. Vi-Fi is now only available in some parts of the world, while more and more places are opting for total isolation. Arcadia was once the exception. Now it is becoming the rule. Even my children have turned their boarding school into an alpine version of my mother's community.

Perhaps biology is destiny. Like cells, we divide and divide again. The recipe for life may end up being our death sentence.

Thank you, @MandelaLives, that's an important question, and I'm glad that you're back with us from Cape Town. What difference does it make in the long run? Our sun will burn out eventually and the universe will dissipate into emptiness. Before that, an asteroid might hit the Earth and wipe out the human race just as an earlier strike doomed the dinosaurs. Even if we manage to avoid self-destruction, something might do the job for us.

Ultimately, this trip goes only one way.
Forget about refunds; there is no return.
How long will it take for us humans to learn
that there's nothing more at the end of the day?

Yet if we can create meaning within the limited tenure of our own lives, then perhaps we can do the same for the longer life span of the species. We set these enormous challenges for ourselves—an immense tower to build, seven great valleys to traverse, a poem of complex form and meter to write, two sons to raise to adulthood—and purpose somehow arises from our struggle to meet such challenges.

If we decide to turn our backs on the tasks we set for ourselves, then suicide is the only option. Which is, of course, the path that Martinson himself took when the Stockholmer cut open his stomach with a pair of scissors four years after winning the Nobel Prize in Literature.

The journey continues and still I must write,
weaving a text that is both fiction and fact,
forever unsure of the final impact,
yet pushing my readers from darkness to light.

The meaning is there, but it's all on the page.
I, not the captain, can determine the path.

It doesn't hinge on engineering or math,
but only the beat of the heart in its cage.

We're still on the run, my brothers and I, along with all the other renegades of Babel. Our parents are dead; my husband is now an ex-husband; my children have cut themselves off from all communication. This is the only family we have. The Abstinents are determined to destroy our tower, to scatter the builders once again to the ends of the earth, and they're aided in those efforts by the White Tigers and the Sleepers. To stop them is a formidable challenge.

Meanwhile, I focus my efforts on this underground academy, which hops from place to place to elude discovery. Our pursuers so far haven't located us without tripping one of the many alarms Karyn has built into the system. She provides us with our only edge. She is a godsend, no doubt, but she isn't a god. She continues to explore her capabilities, which daily surprise us. She can help us, but she can't save us.

I don't know how this cat-and-mouse game will end. All I know is that you are our last great hope. That's why I have delivered these lectures. But now we are done. We have finished the seventh poem. We have passed through the seventh valley, the valley of deprivation and death.

As ever before, there is only one place to turn at this time of crisis.

The answer, my dear friends,
has never been clearer
Who will save us? Just take
a look in the mirror.

Acknowledgments

I want to thank Tom Engelhardt and Nick Turse, who expertly shepherded this trilogy from conception to completion. Ida Audeh provided sharp-eyed and wise copyediting for this volume. The Haymarket team, as always, has added professional design and promotion.

For this final book in the series, I also want to give special thanks to the people who provided invaluable input on Aurora's poems: Mary Amato, Sarah Browning, Jed Feffer, and E. Ethelbert Miller. My dear partner Karin Lee helped improve this novel in immeasurable ways.

By the way, if you would like to read Aurora's poems in full, you can find them at johnfeffer.com/books /songlands/.

ABOUT THE AUTHOR

John Feffer is a playwright and the author of several books including *Splinterlands*, *Frostlands*, and the novel *Foamers*. His articles have appeared in the *New York Times*, the *Washington Post*, the *Nation*, *Salon*, and others. He is the director of Foreign Policy In Focus at the Institute for Policy Studies.